THE SKY'S THE LIMIT.

"Do you realize what I'm offering? Do you know how many men come sniffing around here like coyotes, trying to get it? There are some in town who'd dump their wives and children if I smiled at them the right way. I have to put them off all the time. Think about it, Raider. A fortune and the best lovemaking you'll ever find. What more can a man ask for?" Rina whispered.

"I'll think about it," said Raider. "But not now. We both got better things to do than think."

Then Raider rolled her body hard against his own.

J.D. HARDIN

HELLFIRE HIDEAWAY

BERKLEY BOOKS, NEW YORK

HELLFIRE HIDEAWAY

A Berkley Book / published by arrangement with
the author

PRINTING HISTORY

Berkley edition / April 1983

ISBN: 0-425-06138-8

A BERKLEY BOOK® TM 757,375
The name "BERKLEY" and the stylized "B"
with design are trademarks belonging to
Berkley Publishing Corporation.

PRINTED IN THE UNITED STATES OF AMERICA

CHAPTER ONE

Until the Frenchwoman entered the parlor car, there wasn't much to keep Raider awake. In fact, everything in sight, and in earshot, was designed to put him to sleep. First, there was the landscape, which had changed now that they'd come out of the mountains and the narrow-gauge train was chugging through the broad basin of western Colorado. Here, everywhere you looked was much the same—rolling hills, hard grass, a few outcroppings of rock, and an occasional twisted juniper. It was good cattle country, but enough to bore a dim-witted cow and put such a critter to sleep, too. Then there was the sound of the train on the rails, clickety-clackety, clickety-clackety, over and over again. Finally there was the air, heavy with tobacco smoke, in the car itself.

Doc poked Raider's arm.

"Goddamn it, Rade," said Doc, "are you just going to sit there and sleep all day?"

Raider's eyelids came partly open, as though pried with a lodgepole. His face was strong and leathery, even in this deep repose that bordered on hibernation. His broad, sweeping mustaches seemed to be laid back in sleep too.

Raider grunted. "Huh?"

Doc's face, animated and expressive, rounder and softer than Raider's—at least on the surface—twisted itself into a look of annoyance and disgust. "The least you could do is talk to me about something!" he said.

Raider said, "What the hell for?" and closed his eyes again.

Doc sighed deeply and didn't bother to list all the things that, in his estimation, they might be profitably discussing. Deep down somewhere, he was jealous of Raider's ability to sleep in a saddle or with his head on a hard rock, then come instantly awake when he had to, his fists or his gun cocked and ready to go, if need be. There was a certain disadvantage to this, of course—it gave a man the inclination to shoot first and ask questions afterward. Whereas Doc, more thoughtful, usually did it the other way around. But, on the whole, it was a good way to be out here in the wild, open country where dangers so often came upon you out of nowhere and without any warning. Even the fat diamondbacks, contrary to popular opinion, didn't always rattle before they struck—a bit of lore now well known to Doc Weatherbee, who was a long way, in time and distance, from the streets of New York City where he'd been raised.

Doc continued to scowl at his sleeping partner. The train was almost at its destination now, and they should have been making plans instead of just slouching here on these journey-stained green mohair seats, doing nothing. Which was the way Raider always did things. Doc should have been used to it by now, but he wasn't.

In his own boredom, Doc turned his head slowly to look around the car for perhaps the hundredth time. The passengers, all men, were of a dozen easily identifiable types: businessmen in dark grosgrain, cattlemen in canvas or buckskin, miners in heavy twill—well, you name 'em. One group, near the rear of the car, had swung a seat-back forward to make room for a poker game. Doc had thought of asking to join them, but had decided the conversation would be too dull and the pickings too easy, even for himself, who wasn't a card sharp but was a shade brighter than they looked. It was a kind of curse, being quick-witted. You couldn't just enjoy the company of ordinary folks that way, sometimes. Unless, of course, you were playing a role and had some hidden purpose in mind to keep you entertained—which happened now and then during these operations he and Raider carried out for the agency.

And as Doc looked, idly, unthinkingly, the Frenchwoman entered the car by the rear door. She stepped in, paused, and surveyed the car with a hesitant expression, as though not sure whether or not she really wanted to come in.

Heads turned slowly, and the men in the car, becoming aware of her presence, stared back at her. The buzz of low talk stopped immediately, and there was now only the clickety-clack of the wheels.

Doc had seen her only from a distance before, and now, at closer range, he stared at her in growing appreciation. First, there was the way she was dressed, and this, Doc knew, even though he had little knowledge of high fashion, was definitely French and, as the French themselves might say, decidedly chic. Her dress was of pale green silk with a lace overskirt slanting down from it in front; the tied ribbon devices at shoulder, waist, and thigh Doc seemed to recall were called "hummingbirds," and were considered by women and such to be slightly provocative and daring. More provocative to his eye was the great swelling of her generous bosom, the top halves of which were exposed by the low cut of the dress, so that the rounded line between them was clearly visible. In fact, her bosom was of remarkable size for such a small girl, and the tininess of her waist—which Raider, Doc swore, could have encircled with his hands alone—made it seem even larger.

He wrenched his stare away from her breasts, presently, so that he could take in her face, too. It was a broad oval dominated by two large, round, dark eyes with long lashes that made them seem to sparkle. And on her lower cheek, just to the left of her pouty red lips, there was the single spot of a beauty mark, which he understood was also French fashion, and which did, for some reason, by God, add a kind of sauciness to her overall look.

As he looked, Doc felt himself getting a hard-on.

When he'd glanced at the poker-playing group before, Doc had vaguely noticed the big man with the blunt, somewhat florid face who had kept tilting a pint bottle of redeye, not bothering to offer it to his companions. Showing a loose grin, this man now rose somewhat clumsily, turned his grin full bore upon the young woman, and said in a loud voice, "Hey, little lady! You come right in! You come on in and sit right on my lap here!"

There was laughter from the group—it was a touch nervous.

The girl looked away from the bulky man, deliberately ignoring him.

"Come on, little lady! You hear what I say?" he said. He lurched toward her.

At this, the young woman frowned, glanced toward the man again, and then stepped backward, as though to withdraw from the car. The man, stumbling in the aisle now, reached out as though to grab her.

Doc took a deep breath and was about to trot to the rear of the car and do something about all this. Before he could move, Raider, whom he'd thought was still asleep, propelled himself from his seat, blurred past Doc, and sprang down the aisle in a swift, gliding movement, reaching the girl and the man accosting her before Doc had time to do much more than continue staring.

Raider had a hawk-claw grip on the big man's arm. He looked right into his eyes with a smile on his face. Doc knew that smile. There was so little mirth in it that it almost couldn't be called a smile.

"Partner," said Raider, "I never hit a man when he's drunk. What I do, instead, is squash him right down into the floor. Now, if you figure you wouldn't care to be squashed, you just sit and make yourself quiet as a nice, little old mouse, okay?''

The man was evidently not so drunk that he couldn't sense the steel under Raider's smile and soft words. He stared back only for a moment, and then, with embarrassment, in an attempt to salvage at least a smidgen of his pride, he scowled and said, "Aw, I was only foolin'." Immediately and meekly, he sat down again.

Doc came up to the scene, swaying a little with the movement of the train as he walked, as Raider showed the young woman an almost reluctant suggestion of a bow.

"*Merci*. Thank you," she said to Raider, her eyes big upon him.

"Name's Raider," he said. "At your service, ma'am."

Doc didn't want to be left out of it. He halted as he came abreast of Raider, executed a more proper bow, and swept his pearl gray derby from his head. It was a kind of a rebuke to Raider, who still had his black Stetson raked at a forward angle on his brow—though Doc doubted the taller man caught the subtlety of it. "I'm Doc Weatherbee," said Doc. "Also at your service."

"It is kind of you, m'sieurs," she said. "I will leave now." She started to turn.

"No call for that," said Raider quickly. "You can just keep on goin' wherever it was you were goin'. We'll see nobody bothers you."

She stopped turning and showed a tiny frown. "Well— *eh, bien*—I was on my way to the dining car—"

"Then that there is where we'll go," Raider said. He offered his arm. She looked at it for a moment, then put her hand upon it. Raider swung himself around, and, side by side with him, her head came up only to his broad, yoked shoulder. Raider's smile, cold before, had now become almost pleasant. He looked at Doc, who was in the middle of the aisle. "You gonna move your carcass so's we can get past?" he asked.

Doc scowled back at Raider. "I'll lead the way," he said.

"Ain't no use you comin' along, Doc," said Raider.

"Wouldn't miss it for the world," Doc said, grinning.

Doc spun about and they proceeded forward, the young woman's hand still on Raider's arm. Doc heard them talking behind him.

"I have not introduced myself," he heard the girl say. "I am Claudette Sirois."

"Yeah, I know," Raider grunted.

"How is it that you know?" There was a touch of surprise in her voice.

"Well, it gets around who's on the train," Raider said.

Evidently she accepted that, for there was no more talk until they emerged into the dining car just ahead. There was a kind of vestibule space here, and Doc was able to shuffle himself into place on the other side of the girl. "I take it you want a table, mademoiselle," he said.

"Yes. I thought I would come here to refresh myself just for a change. And it is madame, not mademoiselle."

"That's right, I forgot," Doc said.

"I am surprised; you both seem to know who I am," she said.

"If we may join you," said Doc, "we'll explain—and get better acquainted all around."

Raider glared at Doc. "Who invited *you* in?"

"I did," said Doc. "You're not thinking of uninviting me, are you?"

"We'll see," said Raider, holding his scowl.

A gray-haired Negro attendant in a white coat came forward and, smiling, showed them all to a table near the middle of the car. There was a quick shuffle, during which Raider swiftly managed to slip in beside Claudette so that Doc was forced to take the seat across the table from them. Raider looked at Doc with a tiny ember of triumph in his eye.

"It is not that I wish to dine," said Claudette, arranging herself in her seat.

Doc, slightly more distant from her than Raider was, could catch her heavy perfume, and for some reason it made him start to stiffen again in his trousers. If it did that to him at this distance, he reflected, Raider, right beside her and pressed up against her the way he was, must really be straining.

"Something light—perhaps a glass of wine," she said to the attendant. "It is that you have wine?"

"Yes, ma'am," said the attendant. "Though I'd try the sarsaparilla instead, if I was you."

"You may be right," she said, smiling. "My 'usband and I, we have not found very good wine here in the United States."

"Never liked wine much," said Raider. "The Mexicans make it some. Kinda sweet. Gives you a headache next day."

"Sarsaparilla," she said to the attendant. "And—I don't know—a small piece of cake?"

"All we got is doughnuts, ma'am."

"Very well. Doughnuts."

The attendant scuttled off.

Claudette turned her smile first upon Doc and then upon Raider. "It makes little difference. It was merely the change—to get out and see some people."

"I reckon I know what you mean," said Raider. "Must make you feel cooped up back in that private car. Your husband still there?"

"Armand?" She laughed a little. "Oh, yes. He is busy with his engine drawings, as usual. He is the inventor of many engines, you see, one of which, a fire engine, is on the train—"

"Sure," said Raider. "We know about that, too. Saw the contraption back there on the flat car. We asked about it and that's how we found out who y'all were."

"Ah, that explains it," said Claudette. She primped her

hair absentmindedly, the upward movement of her arms jiggling her breasts a little so that Doc, unable to help himself, had to stare. "But what about you gentlemen? I understand it is not polite, here in the American West, to ask too many questions, yet I am naturally curious."

"Well, as it happens," said Raider. "we're on our way to the same place you are."

"Tamarack Springs?" Her finely plucked eyebrows rose. "Well, that is, how do you say—a coincidence."

"Not really," said Doc, chiming in. "More people going there these days, even if it is off the beaten track. The town's growing, and they're going to make a big cattle center out of it. Which, of course, is why your husband's bringing that fire engine of his, and why Raider and I decided to go there and hang out our shingle."

"Shingle? What is that?"

"It's a way of saying 'going into business.' I'm a veterinarian, you see, and Raider here, he's my prime assistant."

"It's more like we're equal partners," said Raider, evidently not liking to be thought of as anyone's assistant.

"I see," said Claudette, nodding. "Well, at least your profession is interesting. I have always like liked animals. The machines of my 'usband, they become a little dull at times."

"I reckon they do," said Raider, looking at her thoughtfully.

The attendant returned with the news that there were no more doughnuts but there was apple pie, a slice of which he had brought in case she'd like that instead. She said she would, and he set it before her along with the glass of sarsaparilla. She tasted the stuff through a straw, made a face, shrugged, and tasted a little more. "One accepts what is available," she said.

Claudette and Raider now went into a short stretch of small talk that Doc scarcely heard as he quietly contemplated both of them. He was seeing the way Raider was looking at her, and how she was responding with quick glances of her own, and it was evident now that Raider was her choice. Which maybe was just as well. If she'd exhibited equal interest in both men they probably would have had another knock-down-drag-out over it. They'd never managed to find out which was better—Raider's brute force or Doc's tricky elusiveness, and their brawls always left them exhausted and a bit cut up; they really weren't very intelligent, come to think of it, but when pride came to the fore, as it always did, you never did come to think of it.

At times he didn't know why he stuck with Raider the way he did. The big former sodbuster from Arkansas had a million ways to irritate Doc—and Doc supposed it was the same the other way around. Raider wasn't really slow-witted; he sometimes just didn't give a damn. Doc had hastened to explain that they were going to Tamarack Springs as a veterinarian and his assistant so Raider wouldn't absentmindedly change the story, which they needed as cover.

Half listening, as he sat there, Doc soon began to feel which way the wind was blowing as far as Claudette was concerned.

"It is not that I complain about Armand," she was saying. "He is a very good man, and gives me everything I ask for. Perhaps that is because he is a little older and a little sentimental. But his mind is always on those machines of his; he can think about nothing else."

"Not even—uh—at certain times?" asked Raider.

Her smile flickered. "Not even then," she admitted.

Doc knew then that everything was signed, sealed, and delivered. The rest of it was just a matter of making arrangements. He listened as they did exactly that—in a roundabout way, of course. He was a little surprised at how smoothly Raider went along with it. Though he shouldn't have been surprised; what Claudette had to offer was clearly worth a bit of extra effort.

"Must be nice to have your own private car," Raider said.

"Well, it is only part of the private car—a large state-room, so to speak. Armand would have selected a berth for only himself, but he thought I would be comfortable this way. I am, of course, except for a little loneliness."

"That's somethin' I reckon I can take care of for you," said Raider. "No sense in bein' lonely."

"I suppose you yourself are quite comfortable, Raider," she said. Her accent made his name, when she spoke it, sound something like "Red-hair."

"Tell you what," said Raider. "I'll show you where Doc and I hole up. You can see for yourself."

"Why, that would be interesting," she said.

"Sure would," said Raider, his eyes hard upon her.

When she had finished her pie and about a third of her sarsaparilla, and when she and Raider had risen and left—all very casually—Doc stayed in place, ordered coffee, and lit one of his Old Virginia cheroots, which, because of their pungency, were best not smoked in the presence of ladies.

He sat there and watched the rolling, sagebrush hills go by, unchanging. He listened to the steady clickety-clack.

He and Raider knew more about Armand Sirois, the French engineer, than Claudette guessed, though the man's reasons for traveling to Tamarack Springs were peripheral to their own. They'd seen Sirois board the train in Denver, but they hadn't given him a great deal of attention because Claudette had been at his side, and she was the one they'd looked at for the most part. Doc remembered only that Sirois was immensely fat and that he bustled about importantly as though used to having people wait on him.

The chief operative in the Denver office of the Pinkerton National Detective Agency, where Doc and Raider had received their orders, had told them a little about Armand Sirois. He represented the newly founded Compagnie Incendie France-Amérique, which had come up with a steam fire engine to rival those made in America and England; it featured something called a centrifugal pump, which Doc didn't fully understand, but which apparently threw a gushing stream of water more than a hundred feet, which was half again as far as the older-type engines could throw, and which many big cities were now hastening to procure for their own fire departments. He didn't know how the tiny, out-of-the-way town of Tamarack Springs had come up with funds to purchase one of these new engines, but somehow it had, and for some reason—also still unclear—Sirois had decided to deliver it in person. It was Doc's guess he'd promoted himself a trip to the Great American West, which seemed to be attracting a lot of Europeans these days.

Well, the more fire engines Tamarack Springs could afford, the better, thought Doc, and that was another way of saying he didn't really give a hoot. They had an investigation to carry out at the Springs, and it sounded like a fairly dull job this time, one to be finished as quickly as possible so they could get on to their next assignment, hoping it might offer more of a challenge.

It would be nice, he thought, if they could make it back to Chicago, for a change, after this one, and get their orders from Allan Pinkerton in person. Not that they craved his company—he was getting old and crotchety now—but a visit to the big city would be refreshing. Doc knew a couple of places there where the girls were really choice. At one you could get any color you were in the mood for: white, yellow, black, or brown, and varying shades in between.

Thinking about that, he began to swell again down where it counted.

He smiled to himself and drew on his cheroot.

The wheels went clickety-clackety, clickety-clack. . . .

CHAPTER TWO

There was hardly room to roll around in, there in the upper
berth, but that in itself was a challenge that made it more
interesting. Raider thought of something Doc had once
said. He hadn't paid much attention to it at the time, but
now it made sense. One piece of ass, Doc had said, is
essentially the same as any other piece of ass; it's where
you do it and how you work up to it that counts.

Claudette, down to her last flimsy undergarment—a silk
thing that probably had a fancy name—was on her side
and clamped tightly to him. He was fully stripped and his
own lean body, with its whipcord muscles, was bowed
against hers. That last little thing she wore—crumpled way
up now to expose her belly and her thighs—made it more
exciting, oddly enough, than it would have been if she
were thoroughly nude. One of its shoulder straps had
fallen aside, and one huge breast pouted up at him. The
nipple, hardened and rubbery, was centered in an immense
pink disc almost the size of a flapjack, and the skin around
it looked as rich as Guernsey cream. He lowered his mouth
wide open upon it, breathed hot, and licked, and she gasped
with pleasure.

"Do it, Raid-air," she half groaned. "*Mon Dieu!* Do
it!"

"Do what?" he said, half smiling.

17

"Anything!" she said, rolling her eyes. "Everything!"

He palmed her thigh with his hand, then slid it to the grassy nest at the base of her taut, tiny belly. It had the aura of newly turned earth that was mingling now with her heavy perfume. He found the button in its little V-shaped receptacle; like her nipples, it had now hardened so that it protruded almost saucily. When the tip of his finger stroked it she could not contain herself and cried aloud.

"Oh, Raid-*air*!"

She clutched him so tightly now that her fingernails dug into his back like talons.

Raider withdrew his hand and rolled his hips forward to replace it with his oversized, throbbing shillelagh.

"Wait! Not yet!" said Claudette.

Tiny and lithe, she managed, in the narrow berth with its low overhead clearance, to reverse her position with remarkable grace and agility, her breast tips brushing along Raider's body as she did so. In a moment her head was at the level of his hips, and, resting on one elbow, she brought both hands forward to cup his testicles gently, as though she held a sacred offering.

"I will show you what we do in France," she murmured.

"If it's what I think, they do it most anywhere," he said dryly.

Her mouth encircled his cudgel. He felt its hot cavern close over it. She took the entire bulbous head with it and closed her lips softly but firmly on the stem an inch or so below the prepuce. And then, with astonishing agility, her tongue began to flicker all around the blunt knob contained within, lashing and stroking it gently, rubbing a little harder on the sensitive spot just below the head on the underside whenever it touched there.

Raider was not a man to cry aloud with joy over much of anything, but this time he had all he could do to keep from making such a sound. He couldn't remember when anyone had done it this skillfully—and that included more occasions than he could count up right now. If this was common in France, he thought, he'd better go there some-time. Anyway, she was right; it wasn't something you found most anywhere.

When he felt himself beginning to surge, she squeezed his nuggets gently. He braced himself for the explosion.

She drew her head away and let go of his testicles. She laughed. "Not yet, Raid-air!" she said. "Not yet!"

It took all the self-control he could muster to rein him-self in.

Once more she reversed her position, wriggling around until they were again face to face and belly to belly. He looked into her large, long-lashed eyes. "You gonna do that some more?"

"Of course," she said, giggling. "Many times."

It hadn't taken much talk to get her into the upper berth with him. The whole thing had been arranged almost silently, with both knowing very well, from the moment they entered the sleeping car, what was going to happen. All the berths had been made up for the evening, and all those who would occupy them had drifted to other parts of the train, so that the car was deserted. He'd been prepared to send the porter away with a generous tip, but the porter hadn't been on hand either. He'd patted the upper berth with his hand and said, "Wanna try it?" and Claudette had said, without hesitation, "Lift me, please."

She reached down now to bend his member toward the thick patch of hair between her legs, and then, instead of steering it into her quim, she clamped her thighs together upon it.

"It is good to wait," she murmured. "To wait and wait."

"If a feller can," said Raider.

"Ah, you can, Raid-air," she said. "I know you can."

"I'm tryin' " he said, with what was almost a grin, "but it ain't easy."

Her tongue flickered out playfully to the tip of his nose as she squirmed against him slightly. "I have been waiting a long time for someone who can take his time," she said.

"What's that there supposed to mean?"

"Armand," she said. "My 'usband. First, he is much too quick. Second, he does not want to do it very often. It is my fault, I suppose. I knew I was marrying an older man; I knew he thought more of his machines than of pleasing a woman."

"How come you married him, then?"

She shrugged. "He is very rich."

"Good a reason as any, I reckon," Raider said.

Abruptly, she switched herself around again and mouthed Raider as she had before. Once more she brought him to the point of explosion, then broke away. The tingling all through Raider's body made him feel so light and unreal that he had the queer sensation of floating in mid-air, there in the upper berth.

"You are doing very well," she said, when she was facing him again. "It is civilized to prolong the pleasure. And, above all, in France we are civilized."

"If this is bein' civilized," said Raider, his smile twitching rather than spreading itself fully, "I'm all for it." He reached down and tried to maneuver his rod into the hot vestibule between her legs.

"Non! Non!" she said quickly. "Later!"

"Might not have time," he said. "Won't that husband of yours be lookin' for you?"

"Not Armand. He is studying his plans for that stupid fire engine again. The world could come to an end and he would not know it."

"Heard about that engine. How come a small place like Tamarack Springs is gettin' one?"

Claudette shrugged. "I do not know exactly. Perhaps I do not listen closely enough when Armand talks about it. I think the people in this town are expecting it to grow. The railroad, I believe, is going to run a line to it. Something like that. They now have a fire chief—one M'sieur Ormsby.

He will take delivery of the engine, and Armand, I suppose, will show everyone how to use it. And there is some rich woman who, I believe, has paid for most of it. Her name is Larkin, and she owns a ranch. It is Armand's business, and theirs, and I do not care much about it.''

"Right now," said Raider, "I don't either. Come on, let's get down to cases."

"In a little while," said Claudette, laughing. "First, I will bring you to the edge again."

A third time she wrigged herself about and her head descended upon his groin. She mouthed and licked him even more furiously this time, and several times she herself shuddered as her own excitement brought her to her first, early orgasms.

Raider was certain he could no longer hold himself in. There was nothing he could do now but let himself go, then work up a new one. With Claudette here squirming all over him and gobbling at his member as it never had been gobbled at before, that shouldn't take too long. What the hell, she wanted to put it off as long as possible, anyway.

He was about to release everything. It was a split-second away. . . .

From somewhere outside the train, there came the sound of gunfire.

In the dining car, where he still sat staring at the landscape, Doc had seen the riders as they drew abreast of the train and at first had thought not much in particular about them. On a slight upward grade now, the train was chugging along a little more slowly, and it was common for cowhands, when a train came by, to race along with it for a while—maybe to prove what most of them fondly believed: that snorting machines like trains would never really replace the horse as a reliable means of transportation.

He watched them idly at first, then cocked his head and frowned a little as they edged nearer the train. A moment later, he saw that all six of them had bandanas drawn up to just below their eyes to conceal their faces.

That was when Doc butted his nearly finished cheroot in the ashtray and rose quickly. The Negro attendant was near the rear of the car, also staring curiously out the window. Doc called to him. "Where's the conductor?"

"Up forward," said the black man, waving in that direction. His alarmed expression said that he knew as well as Doc did what was about to happen.

Doc rushed forward and into the next car. He had scarcely entered it when he bumped into the conductor, who was coming aft. Doc barred his way. "You see what's out there?"

The conductor was a thin, middle-aged man who wore steel-rimmed spectacles. "I see it!" he said. "Can't figure what they're up to!"

"They're up to robbing this train, that's what they're up to," said Doc.

"Nothin' on it to rob!" said the conductor. "No money shipments, no mail—nothin' like that. That's why we ain't got a guard!"

"Well, maybe they're after whatever the passengers might have on them," Doc said. "Anyway, you've got a guard now. Me and my partner." He looked around quickly to be sure no one was within earshot. "We're Pinkerton operatives."

The conductor's eyebrows rose in surprise for a moment. Then he hauled them down again and said, "Okay. Do whatever you have to. It there gonna be shootin'?"

"Wouldn't be surprised," said Doc.

"Go ahead, then," said the conductor. "I'm gettin' out o' the way!"

Doc was already visualizing the defensive tactics he and Raider would need. "The flatcars in the rear," he said quickly. "We'll work from there. Can we get to 'em?"

"Door's locked," said the conductor. "Come on, I'll open it for you. Then I *am* disappearin'!"

As Doc and the conductor were pushing their way aft, the shooting started outside. The attackers were forward, abreast of the locomotive, and Doc couldn't see them, but it was his educated guess that what he heard was a series of warning shots designed to make the engineer stop the train. This was confirmed a moment later when the train jolted and began to lose speed.

Both men now entered the sleeping car. Doc glanced at Raider's upper berth, saw the drawn curtain, and said to the conductor, "Keep going! I'll be with you in a minute!"

The conductor disappeared down the corridor, and Doc reached up and pulled the curtain open. The first thing he saw was the creamy expanse of Claudette's bare and beautiful ass staring him in the face—near enough for him to lean forward and kiss it, if he'd had a mind to, and, truth was, that occurred to him in passing. Raider's face glared at him from just over the line of Claudette's curvaceous waist.

"Bandidos, partner," said Doc calmly. "Better throw something on."

Claudette twisted herself around to stare at him angrily. "How dare you!" she cried, clumsily trying to bring her undergarment up to cover herself at least partly.

"Sorry, ma'am," said Doc calmly. "Make it snappy, Raider."

"Goddamn!" said Raider. "You could have knocked or somethin'!" He was already twisting himself around to struggle into his trousers.

"Raid-air!" cried Claudette. "Make this man go away!"

"Wish I could, Sugar," said Raider.

In a moment he was on the floor, slipping into his boots. He took another moment to find his gunbelt in his valise, and Doc reached into his own berth to do the same. Raider strapped his heavy .44 low on his rough twill pants quickly enough; Doc took an extra second or two to affix his own Colt Diamondback .38 with its shorter, four-inch barrel under the jacket of his fancy mouse-gray suit.

Raider glanced at him in disgust—it was no time for a man to be worrying about how he looked.

Then, together, they rushed toward the rear of the train, Raider naked from the waist up, Doc's coattails flying. Claudette, holding a sheet up to her neck, stared after them in astonishment.

The conductor was already at the opened door of the last passenger car when they arrived. Beyond him they could see the flatcar on which Monsieur Sirois's fire engine, held down by cables, stood, and beyond that the first of two freight cars, which contained several horses and Doc's mule, Judith who he hoped, hadn't kicked down the partition between herself and the horses by now. The second and rearmost freight car held Doc's wagon, which had been repainted with lettering announcing veterinary services instead of the medicinal nostrums he usually purveyed as a cover to explain his presence wherever he went.

Raider and Doc scrambled onto the flatcar, and the conductor slammed the door shut behind them. Then, as he'd promised, he made himself scarce.

The train had been slithering along, brakes grinding, and now it was almost halted. "Good place, here," said Doc, pushing along toward the partial concealment of the fire engine. "They'll go through the passenger cars, and we'll get the drop on 'em when they come out and won't be expecting it."

"How the hell do you know what they're gonna do?" growled Raider.

"Matter of probabilities," said Doc smugly.

"Shee-it!" said Raider. Doc's little sorties into logic and philosophy and that sort of thing always irritated him—as did a number of Doc's other habits.

The train jolted sharply as it halted completely. Both Raider and Doc grabbed at the fire engine for support to keep from being thrown forward. It was a funny-looking machine, in a way—basically a steam boiler set on a big-wheeled carriage, with a whiffletree for a four-horse team up front. The boiler and all its valves and pipes were shining brass; the rest of it was painted bright red with golden curlicue decoration here and there. Atop the boiler was a huge brass eagle and, on each side, a metal plaque bearing the crossed flags of France and the United States.

Raider touched Doc's arm and nodded toward the front of the train. "You guessed wrong, Doc. They're comin' this way."

Doc stared. Sure enough, two of the riders had mounted the locomotive, and the other four, still on their horses, were trotting back toward the flatcar.

"I'll be goddamned," said Doc.

"Guess you will," said Raider. "Sooner or later."

"I don't expect they're after this fire engine—"

"Best you don't expect anything," said Raider. "Stop tryin' to think so much, and take what comes, that's all." Raider drew his .44. "Okay, let's give 'em their little surprise."

"Wait. First, let's see what they're after."

"What's the difference? Thing to do is drive 'em off, whatever they're after."

"Hold on just a second, Rade," said Doc. "Bear with me."

The four riders were almost up to the flatcar now. The one in the lead—a rangy man who rode in a kind of slouch—switched around in his saddle briefly and called to the others, "Here she is, boys! Luke, you got that dynamite?"

One of the men behind him waved a bundle of explosives.

"They're fixing to blow up the fire engine!" said Doc, in astonishment. "What the hell for?"

"Who cares what the hell for," said Raider. "Okay, Doc—let 'em have it!"

Raider got off the first shot. Doc knew he hadn't meant to hit the rangy rider with it, because if he had the man would have dropped. As it was, Doc suspected the rider must have heard the bullet buzz past his head; at this distance, Raider could put a slug pretty much where he wanted it.

The lead rider's horse reared, almost throwing him. The men behind him pulled their own horses to a halt in great surprise and confusion. Doc sighted along the slit-topped barrel of his own stubby Diamondback and, not as dead a shot as Raider, aimed wide to the right of the second rider. He must have done all right, because at the sound of the report this man's horse also reared and then danced off to one side as he fought to control it.

The third rider, a gun already in his hand, squeezed off a shot in their general direction. They heard the bullet strike the fire engine somewhere with a loud *thunk!* and then go off somewhere else in a whistling ricochet.

"Okay, you polecats!" called Raider. "One more like that and you're all buzzard meat!"

For emphasis, he sent another shot toward them.

The four riders took another moment to glance at each other wildly—none, obviously, knowing quite what to do next.

"Skedaddle!" yelled Raider. "Haul your asses outa here!"

That seemed to help them make up their minds. The lead rider wheeled around, kicked his horse with his heels, and went off at a slant toward the front of the train and away from it. In the next second, the other riders did the same and followed him. Moments later, the men who had gone into the locomotive cab scrambled back on their horses and larruped away in the wake of the other four. Within minutes, all six had disappeared over a low rise, leaving a trail of settling dust behind them.

Raider blew at the muzzle of his gun to clear away smoke he must have imagined was there. Dumb, the way he sometimes did that after shooting, Doc thought.

Doc now looked at him in deep disgust. "Well, Rade," he said, holstering his own weapon, "you fucked it up again."

"What?" said Raider, glaring at Doc.

"You should've held 'em here long enough for us to find out what they were after."

"They were after this contraption," said Raider, nodding at the fire engine. "You heard 'em say it."

"Yes, but why? What good does it do anybody to blow up a fire engine?"

"Damned if I know," said Raider, "and damned if I care."

"That's the trouble with you," said Doc. "You don't look for answers."

"The trouble with *you*," retorted Raider, "is you ask too many damn-fool questions."

"Damn-fool, is it?" said Doc, stiffening, drawing himself up. "Use your head, Rade. Might have something to do with why we're here. There's a connection somewhere. I can feel it."

"Balls," said Raider.

"Look at it logically," Doc persisted. "The Philadelphia Contributorship, founded by Ben Franklin in 1752, and still a pioneer in the field of insurance against fire, disaster, and other hazards—"

Raider exploded. "Philadelphia? Ben Franklin? What the fuck's that got to do with it?"

"Lemme tell it my way," snapped Doc. "And stop interrupting. Philly Contrib, as they call it, opens a new Denver office, since they decided to expand west with the rest of the country. A lot of new towns are opening up, and they send drummers out to write 'em up for fire insurance. The Chicago fire in 'seventy-one has got everybody thinking about it, and the time is ripe. Philly's got a new deal where they insure not just one building but the whole town, which figures out cheaper for the individual; they do it by a special tax levy, and the property owner hardly feels the bite. Claims are paid to the town itself, which, in turn, reimburses the party or parties who suffered a fire loss."

"If I wanted to know all this," grumbled Raider, "I'd of been an insurance drummer with a stickpin and a hat like yours. Which, thank God, I ain't."

"Then try to understand this much. No sooner did Tamarack Springs get its policy than there was a rash of fires. Three in a row. When that happens the insurance company sends out an investigator before they pay off. First thing he tries to find out is if there really was a fire. If there was, he figures how much damage was done, so the company knows how much to pay. And the next thing he looks hard for is evidence that maybe the fire was set deliberately by somebody who wanted money more than the property that got damaged. If it was, the law says the company doesn't have to pay up, and that's what they really like. There's one thing about an insurance company. If it can welsh on its bet, it will."

"Uh-huh," said Raider, and Doc wondered if he was really listening. "They told us all this in Denver. What do you have to repeat it for?"

"So it'll sink through that thick skull of yours, that's why. The Philly Contrib hasn't got enough investigators out west and they engaged the Pinkerton Agency, which has men in the area, namely you and me. And here we are."

"It still don't explain why somebody might be after that fire engine."

"Well, like I say," said Doc, frowning, "that part of it's not crystal clear yet, but I can make a few good guesses. Insurance is cheaper if the town's got a fire engine, especially one of these new French kinds that are supposed to be so good, so I expect that's why they bought it in spite of the expense. But if somebody *wanted* fires—somebody who would benefit from an insurance payoff—that same person would want the fire engine out of the way. It just might make a difference in putting out a fire before it really got started."

"Doc," said Raider, "all this is hangin' on too many maybes.' Right now I got other things to think about."

"Like what?"

"Like findin' out where that little French gal got to, and takin' up where we left off. The way you come bargin' in, Doc, interruptin' the way you did, well, goddamn it, I never *did* get my rocks off!"

CHAPTER THREE

On the bulkhead of one of the passenger cars, the Denver & Rio Grande narrow-gauge railway had hung a map showing the locations they serviced in Colorado and in portions of some of the neighboring territories. This map contained a dot that was labeled Yancy, but it was a safe bet no other map in the world did.

Raider and Doc stood in the middle of what some folks in these parts probably wishfully called the main street of Yancy. It was a patch of dust more than it was a street, and it lay between the single track of the railroad and a line of widely spaced frame shacks that could also, by stretching the word, be called buildings.

"There's no such thing as ghosts," said Doc, looking around, "but if there were, they'd live here."

"Now what the hell kind of a statement is that?" said Raider, frowning at him.

"Someday," said Doc, his shoulders rising and falling with the suggestion of a sigh, "I'm going to get me a partner who knows a joke when he hears one."

Raider's frown only deepened. He looked toward the line of frame buildings, none of which had so much as a board sidewalk in front of it. At the far end was the largest structure, a small, two-story house with a sign that said HOTEL. It was the only place with a hitching rail in front of it, though there were no horses, let along the loungers you usually saw in front of a hotel.

A fly buzzed its way to Raider's cheek, and he slapped at it with annoyance. The sun was glaring down at them, trying to turn them into dust, too, for all Doc knew. The midday quiet in the town was almost a soft purr.

"Ain't hardly a fit place for lizards," said Raider, still making a general survey of the scene. "And it looks like that French gal and her fat husband are gonna have to spend the night here. Unless somebody comes to get 'em pretty quick."

Doc nodded. "Whoever's meeting them probably won't be along for a while. The train was early. Like that conductor told me, it's never on time—either early or late."

"I'm thinkin' we might spend the night here too," said Raider, glancing back at the hotel again.

Doc smiled a little. "Figured you'd get an idea like that. Then, as soon as M. Sirois starts snoring, Claudette slips away and comes to your room. That what you had in mind?"

Raider scowled. "Somethin' wrong with it?"

"Well," said Doc, "first off, we're supposed to get to Tamarack Springs quick as we can, do the job, and get the hell out again. Second, while you're rollin' around in bed with Claudette, what am I supposed to do? Bunghole one of the lizards?"

"You can jack yourself off for all I care," said Raider. He nodded at the small building in front of them. "It says 'restaurant.' Let's go eat."

"That, for a change, is a practical suggestion," said Doc.

They stalked toward the tiny restaurant, their boots scuffling up the yellow dust. Behind them, near the fat pipe of the waterspout that was the principal reason for the so-called town of Yancy's existence, stood Doc's veterinary wagon, now unloaded. Judith, his mule, was tethered next to it, idly munching at the small pile of alfalfa that had been brought along for her. And a little beyond the wagon, also unloaded from the flatcar by means of a ramp, stood the bright red fire engine M. Sirois was delivering to Tamarack Springs, still sixty miles away.

After taking on water and sitting for twenty minutes or so while the vehicles had been unloaded, the train had pulled away and puffed off into the distance. After it had left, Yancy had seemed quieter and lonelier than ever. By that time, Sirois had waddled into the hotel, Claudette dutifully coming along a step behind him, and Doc and Raider had wandered the short distance down the dusty main street to kill the time while they decided exactly what to do next.

Raider was hardly in a cheerful mood. After the attack on the train, Sirois—flustered and alarmed, like most of the passengers—had emerged from his stateroom and kept himself at Claudette's side from then on. Amused, Doc saw Raider and Claudette glance at each other helplessly. Their business, if it could be called that, would have to remain unfinished for a while.

Sirois himself had been cordial to Raider. He had shaken his hand, and then Doc's, puffed out his fat, little lips the way he did when he spoke, and said gravely, "M'sieurs, I am in your debt. It was brave of you to defend my engine as you did."

"Wasn't much trouble," said Raider, shrugging.

Doc had looked at him curiously. "Why do you suppose anybody would want to blow up that contraption of yours, like they were fixing to do?"

"Why? *Pourquoi?*" His shrug was heavy and expressive. "I do not know, monsieur. I simply do not know. But no matter, now. You have saved it. M'sieurs, if it should happen that we meet again, in some civilized place, I hope I can treat you to an elegant meal. I will myself oversee the preparation of it and, of course, choose the wine. Indeed, if ever you get to Le Havre, I will cook it myself.

I can promise you, it will be more than a meal. It will be an occasion.''

"Sounds fine," said Raider, looking puzzled and a little doubtful.

Claudette flashed a smile. "It is not an empty promise, M. Raid-air. When Armand prepares a meal, it is worth traveling all the way to France for.''

"Don't know about travelin' that far just for a square meal," said Raider, smiling slightly, "but I can think of other things that might make it worthwhile."

"Oui," said Claudette, with a significance her husband failed to detect.

Now, as they headed for the restaurant, Doc glanced at Raider's frown and, knowing the reason for it, chuckled a little. "You know, Rade," he said, "you could offer 'em a ride on the wagon. It's sixty miles, and I expect you and the gal would find a few chances to slip away before we got there."

"Already made the offer," Raider grunted. "The lard-ass Frenchman said he'd wait for his reception committee. Couldn't make him budge on that."

Doc laughed. "Looks like you just crapped out then. Cheer up. There might be something to dip your wick in at Tamarack Springs—if you can wait that long."

They entered the restaurant. It was a small room with four tables, all empty at the moment. The walls were decorated with brightly colored Mexican serapes, hung like tapestries, a couple of broad-brimmed Jalisco sombreros, and several strings of bright red chile peppers.

There was a counter with a kitchen behind it, and at its far end sat a tall, thin young woman in a calico dress. She had evidently been busy writing in a composition book. In spite of the tiny establishment's decor, she did not look to be of Spanish descent, which Doc figured to be just as well because he wasn't in the mood for burning out the lining of his mouth this morning. He took note of the long, straight red hair that fell to below her shoulders and that was held in place by a cloth band tied Indian fashion around her forehead. As she saw them, she removed a pair of narrow, silver-rimmed glasses from the bridge of her nose and set them down on the counter.

"Gentlemen, good afternoon," she said. "I'll be with you very soon."

Raider nodded. "Whatta you got to eat?"

"Ham and eggs and 'taters fried, much enjoyed by all who've tried," she said.

Doc cocked his head. "You always talk that way?"

"If you mean in rhyme, yes—all the time," said the young woman blithely. She rose, and they saw that she was even taller than she'd looked to be sitting. At first glance she had appeared somewhat bony, but they saw now that there was a certain willowy grace in the way she moved.

Doc laughed. "Never heard the like of it. Well, if ham and eggs is what you've got, that's what we'll have." He shuffled a chair away from a table and he and Raider sat down.

"Rest yourselves and plan to stay," she said. "Coffee comin', right away."

As she poured from a pot that was kept warm on a woodstove, Doc grinned at Raider. Raider's lips relaxed a little, which was his way of grinning, and he grunted once, which was his way of saying, yes, the girl's poetry was one of the goddamnedest things he ever heard.

In a moment the young woman was setting thick, steaming mugs of coffee in front of them.

"Welcome to Yancy. Nothin' fancy," she said. "You two just passin' through? That's all that most folks do."

"On our way to Tamarack Springs," said Doc. "I'm surprised to find this much of a town here. I figured there'd be a water tower and not much else."

"Well, I'll grant you it's not a lot," she said, "but we're satisfied with what we've got. Only trouble is gettin' lonely. And that's on account o' my one and only."

"I don't think I follow you." Doc was inspecting her even more closely now. At first glance he'd decided she was much too tall for him to get interested in, but now, suddenly, she was looking more attractive. Her graceful, feminine way of moving took away from what might have been gawkiness. He saw a hidden frown cross her brow, like something stirring in a patch of underbrush. He knew, even before she spoke again, that whatever was in her mind now was bothersome enough to make her forget the poetry, at least for the moment.

"My name's Virtue, gentlemen," she said, her expression now quite serious as she looked not directly at them but off to one side and somehow into the distance. "Virtue Morgan. My husband is Joe Morgan, and he works for the railroad. He's a brakeman, and they've got him on another line right now, which means he's hardly ever here." Abruptly, she broke from her apparent reverie. "Some would kill the time with curses; I make it pass by writing verses. Relax yourself and stretch your legs, while I go make your ham and eggs."

Doc was still laughing after she had pirouetted away to prepare their meal. Raider looked at him and said, "What's so funny?"

"Not exactly funny. Just—well—remarkable. The way she gets off those rhymes."

"Seems to me she's takin' a lot of trouble for nothin'."

"Don't you like poetry?"

"Sure. Ever hear the one that goes, 'There once was a man from Kentuck', who found hisself down on his luck—' "

"I heard it," said Doc. "And that's not the kind o' poetry I mean. I'm just thinking about this poor lonely gal, stuck out here in the middle of nowhere, her husband away all the time, and maybe not doing her much good when he *does* get home—well, I find her very interesting."

"I find her kinda skinny," said Raider.

Doc shrugged. "Each man to his own taste. But you got to admit this whistle-stop is like being at the end of the world. The only real importance Yancy's got is as a jumping-off place for Tamarack Springs, until they build the spur, if they ever get around to it. I heard all about it from the conductor on the train."

"Why'n hell didn't they run the railroad through Tamarack Springs in the first place," Raider asked.

"No reason to at the time. You see, it's just lately they got serious about raising cattle up there. Before, the Springs was not much more'n an outlaw hideaway."

Raider nodded. "Heard about that. Somebody on the owl hoot could hole up there a spell and not be bothered, 'long as he didn't make no trouble in the town itself."

"It's still that way," said Doc, "but they've got big plans to make it a real cattle-producing center instead, as soon as the railroad builds the spur. That's why they're doing all these things like getting insurance and buying fire engines."

"Well, speakin' of the Springs," said Raider, "we better figure on how to get there. If we start now we'll be on the trail all night. Might be better to leave tomorrow morning and figure on two days flat with a stopover when it gets dark."

Doc grinned. "You'd still like another chance with that French gal in the hotel tonight, wouldn't you?"

"Somethin' wrong with that?" asked Raider sharply.

Virtue was coming back to their table, carrying plates of bread and butter. Her smile was mostly on Doc. He looked up and showed a smile of his own. When he answered Raider's question he was still looking at her. "No, nothing wrong, I guess," he said. "As a matter of fact I'm beginning to think staying over might not be such a bad idea."

The moon was high over the rolling, hard-grassed hills. The stars sparkled, and there almost seemed more of them than there was blue-black sky around them. The town of Yancy—if it could be called a town—lay dead and still in the soft, waxen light.

Virtue's bedroom was in the back of the restaurant. The lace curtains on the window had been pulled apart, and the moonlight streamed into the room. To Doc's eye, Virtue looked better than ever as she stood before him, naked in the moonlight.

Doc, also naked, was stretched out on the bed. She stood tall, at the side of the bed, smiling down at him. Her body rose in a willowy column, and her straight red hair, freed of the restraining band, plunged down on all sides like a coppery cascade. Reaching her breasts, it covered them partly so that the hardened nipples peeked through it at Doc. Farther down, at the base of her long, flat belly, was the inviting triangle of her pubic hair, also fiery red.

"You just lie still," said Virtue in a melodious whisper. "Let me do everything."

"You forgot to rhyme that," said Doc.

"Rhyming's for when I'm lonely," she said. "I'm not, now."

She began to sway and gyrate, deliberately tantalizing his eyes. Her long, lithe body rippled sinously as though its bones were as soft and malleable as the flesh that surrounded them. She smiled when she saw how his member rose; she stretched herself facedown upon him, bending the whip handle down so that it was squeezed between their bellies, and then, in this position, she continued to writhe and rub, massaging Doc with her entire body.

"Jumpin' sassafras!" said Doc in glee. "Where'd you learn to do it like this?"

"In my dreams, it seems," she murmured.

And the rest of it was much like a dream, her gyrations maddening Doc to the point where he wasn't thinking clearly about much of anything and, frankly, preferring it that way. She brought him to his first climax quickly, then immediately began to squirm all over him again until he was ready for seconds. The seconds turned into thirds and fourths. The pale-honey moon moved across the sky and Doc lost count.

Now the pauses between their peaks of delight began to lengthen. But the pauses themselves were pleasure as they lay there side by side.

"I want you to know, Doc," said Virtue quietly, "that I don't do this all the time. I mean . . . when I saw you . . . and you saw me . . . well, there was something about it that was just right. I know you'll be leaving in the morning and maybe we'll never see each other again. But we'll have had this much; the both of us. It'll make it easier for me to put up with everything when Joe drops in again. You have to understand the way it is with me and Joe."

Doc frowned a little. "Not exactly my business—"

"But it's important you know why I needed you, Doc. I was very young when I met Joe Morgan about a year ago and I thought I was in love with him. As I found out later, he was making a special effort to be nice. And he's not a bad-looking man. That's his picture over there."

Doc looked where she had pointed at the far wall. A framed photograph, not too visible in the dim light, showed a man of about forty or a bit less posing stiffly in a black suit with a flowing cravat at his starched collar. He had wide cheekbones, deep-set eyes, and a broad, drooping mustache. What looked like a long scar extended from the corner of his mouth across his cheek, though this, thought Doc, might be some sort of trick shadow captured by the photograph. But he was, as Virtue had said, not bad-looking. Not handsome or anything; just not bad-looking in a plain sort of way.

"Well," said Doc, "as long as we never cross trails I reckon we'll get along."

"It's not that he's been mean with me or anything like that," Virtue went on. "But he ignores me as though I didn't exist, even when he's home—which is hardly ever. We never do—uh—what you and I have just been doing. It took me a while to figure it out, but now I know why he married me and brought me here."

"Why?" Doc asked the question as much to fill the pause as anything.

"All he wanted was a base—some permanent place to be all set up whenever he needed it. Not much more than a permanent address to keep his things and get his mail and everything. His real life is on the railroad, where he keeps moving. And he wanted me here as no more than a housekeeper or a maid; somebody to hold the place down for him. He bought the little restaurant to help pay the upkeep and maybe to keep me busy enough not to complain or walk out on him. I've thought about walking out many times, but"—she sighed—"where would I go? I don't know, Doc. I may still fly the coop one of these days. If I ever get the courage."

Doc laid a hand lightly on her breast. "You're one sweet gal, Virtue, and I wish I could help. I'd be lying to you if I said I could. But my plans just don't call for any hitching arrangement. If I gave you the idea they did, I didn't mean to, and I'm sorry."

"It's all right, Doc," she said. "I understand."

She rolled on top of him and began to writhe again.

Doc emerged from the little frame house at dawn and headed down the dusty main street for the hotel. He was exhausted and felt as though he walked on mist. As he approached the hotel, he saw half a dozen horses tethered to the hitching rail in front of it. Before he could enter the small hostelry, Raider, fully dressed, came barging out of the door.

Raider glared at Doc. "Where the hell you been?"

"Where do you think I've been?" Doc countered. "Taking a poetry lesson."

"Well, get the wagon ready. We're movin' out. The escort for the fire engine got here, and they're headin' back to Tamarack Springs right away. Seems somebody got the date and time fucked up—which figures—and that's what delayed 'em."

"Why do we have to move out with 'em? I could use a little sleep. Maybe even a bath if this hole-in-the-wall's got one."

"Goddamn it, Doc," said Raider. "Just do like I say, okay? We gotta get up to the Springs soon as possible."

"Let me guess," said Doc, staring back at his partner evenly. "You couldn't get together with Claudette last night and you've still got a powerful hard-on. You're figuring on getting to her on the trail."

"Never mind all that. You gonna help get the wagon ready, or am I gonna ride on alone?"

"Okay, damn it," said Doc, sighing deeply. "Let's saddle up."

They were backing a reluctant Judith up to the wagon when two of the riders who had arrived at the hotel came by, mounted, moving their horses at a slow walk toward the fire engine. Doc and Raider paused to look at them as they approached. The man in the lead was whipcord lean and rode lightly, his butt molded to the saddle. He wore a low-crowned black hat and his face was sharp in front, like a well-honed ax. His eyes, which kept moving as though looking for trouble, were set somewhat close together, and his weather-tanned face was filled with a number of deep pockmarks. While he was still out of earshot, Raider nudged Doc and whispered, "That's Dan Carver, the town marshal at the Springs."

Doc looked thoughtful. "Seems to me I heard the name before."

"Right," said Raider. "Gunslinger up Kansas way some years ago. Lawman now. S'posed to be, anyway."

The man riding with Carver was older and heavyset, with a Lincoln-style beard that was almost pure white. His lips seemed set in a permanent half smile, and his eyes looked as though his mind was never exactly where *he* was at any given time; as though he were constantly dreaming of something better or more interesting than whatever was on hand.

"Ab Ormsby, the fire chief," said Raider.

Raider stepped forward as the two men drew abreast.
"We'll have this wagon ready in a jiffy, Marshal," he said.
"If y'all will be kind enough to wait for us."

Carver brought his horse to a halt and frowned down at
Raider. "Dally in a moment here, mister. Do I take it
you're studyin' on ridin' along with us?"

"That there's the idea," said Raider. "Thought you
understood."

Carver's frown deepened. "Sorry to disappoint you,
mister. We'd just as soon not have company."

"What's this, now?" Raider cocked his head slightly.
"You tellin' me you can't use a coupla extra hands, in
case somethin' happens on the way?"

"I'm tellin' you," Carver said evenly, "that we don't
want strangers around while we move this fire engine. Not
accusin' you of anything—it's just that we feel more comfortable with nobody else gettin' near it. I hear somebody
already tried to blow it up. Whoever it is might be figurin'
on another try."

Ab Ormsby edged his horse forward and blinked mildly
at Carver. "Let 'em come along, Dan. Can't see the harm
in it."

"That's 'cause you can't see the harm in much of
anything, Ab," Carver said acidly. "I been appointed to
get this fire engine back to town safe and sound, so I
reckon you just better let me do it my way."

"But I understand these fellers drove off those gunhands
who came after the engine. We owe 'em something," said
Ormsby.

"We don't owe 'em diddledy-shit," snapped Carver.

Glancing at Raider, Doc saw the cold, almost expressionless look Raider always got when something gave him
a burr in his craw. "You ain't exactly showin' real hospitality, Marshal, like they do most places. Seems to me if
we decide to just tag along behind somewheres, there ain't
much you can do about it."

Carver stared back silently for a moment. Then he said, "You want to tag along, go ahead. Maybe you'll find out what I can do about it." He lifted his reins, as though to push on, then seemed to have an afterthought and swiveled his eyes upon Doc and Raider again. "Don't seem to place you two," he said. "What's your business in Tamarack Springs?"

"It's what you just said," Raider answered immediately. "*Our* business."

"Gonna be like that, huh? Well, that's gettin' off on the wrong foot. You must know about the Springs. You must know how—uh—strangers are supposed to check in with me or Mr. Brent when they get there. Anybody who forgets to do that finds he can't stick around very long."

"Don't know what you're talkin' about, Marshal," Raider said blandly. "Who's Mr. Brent?"

Carver's eyes narrowed. "You must be joshin' me."

Raider held his hand up as though taking an oath and said with an air of innocence, "Hope to die."

"I wouldn't do that," Carver said. "You might get your wish quicker'n you think. And you ain't answered my question yet. How come you're headin' for the Springs?"

Knowing that Raider was riled up inside and wouldn't answer just to be stubborn about it, Doc stepped forward and waved at the wagon. The new paint and lettering on it was still bright and fresh. "If you'll take a good look, Marshal," he said, "you'll see who we are. I'm Doc Weatherbee, a practical veterinarian, and Raider here's my assistant. With this wagon we can treat everything from keck to catfits. We heard the animal population in Tamarack Springs wasn't getting proper medical care, so we decided to supply it."

"Hey, that's first rate!" said Ormsby, blinking. "With all the herds growin' the way they are, we can sure use a vet up at the Springs."

"Maybe," growled Carver. "A real vet, maybe."

"You doubtin' our word, Marshal?" asked Raider icily.

"Mister," Carver said, "it's my job to doubt everybody's word. The sooner you get that into your head, the better you'll get along at the Springs." He shifted slightly in the saddle. "If you get there."

The marshal nudged his horse, and it started off again at a walk toward the fire engine by the railroad track. Ab Ormsby showed a passing smile. "Don't mind Carver, gents," he said. "He's spooky 'bout everybody new. Got reason to be. Lotta strangers who pull in to Tamarack Springs are a step ahead o' some bounty hunter. But we're gonna change that, too. Takes a little time, but we'll change it."

"We wish you nothing but luck in your endeavors," said Doc, getting almost courtly about it.

Raider threw a brief, sour look in his direction, as he always did when Doc got fancy that way. Once more, Raider addressed Ormsby. "Who's this here Brent feller the marshal mentioned?"

"Winfield Brent," said Ormsby. "Owns the Grand Palace hotel and saloon. He—uh—kind of arranges things for strangers who blow in."

"Arranges just what?"

"I expect you'll find out all about it when you get there," said Ormsby. "And, by the way, if you want someplace to stay, look me up at the new firehouse. I reckon I can steer you on to somethin' better'n cheaper than the Grand Palace. Well, no time to sit here all day wagglin' my jaws. See you up at the Springs."

When the fire chief had ridden off to catch up with Carver, Doc turned a thoughtful look in Raider's direction. "Not exactly a good start, rubbing the marshal's fur the wrong way, like you just did," he said.

"He was the one doin' the rubbin'," growled Raider,

"not me. Anyway, there's somethin' queer about the whole setup. Don't know pree-cisely what it is, but things just don't smell right."

"This," said Doc, "is one of those rare occasions on which I am in absolute agreement with you."

CHAPTER FOUR

Doc and Raider sat on the high seat of the medicine wagon, or what, at any rate, had been a medicine wagon before its present new coat of paint and fancy lettering that now proclaimed it to be the traveling clinic of one Doc Weatherbee, Practical Veterinarian, as he styled himself. In the past, the two Pinkerton operatives had often used the cover of itinerant medicine men, and the wagon's logo had advertised Doc Weatherbee's Medicinal Wonders, but this time Doc, for some reason incomprehensible to Raider, and maybe not quite clear to Doc, either, had wanted a change of pace and had decided to appear in Tamarack Springs as an animal doctor.

"What if you really have to doctor some critters?" Raider had asked doubtfully.

"I am quite familiar with veterinary medicine," Doc had replied calmly. "I once served an apprenticeship with a very famous practitioner. His wife was a remarkably comely Indian squaw, and the only reason I left him was that he caught us together in bed one night."

"Doc," Raider said, "if you'd done half the things you say you'd done, you'd have to be a hundred years old to get 'em all in."

"I assure you," Doc answered, "that whatever I tell you of my experience is the gospel truth. I learn quick."

Raider grunted and let it go at that.

About a quarter mile ahead of them, the fire engine rolled and bounced slowly on the dirt road, drawn by two horses. Claudette Sirois, bundled up in a linen duster, sat on its seat beside the driver, turning around now and then to peer at the wagon and the two men who followed the fire engine procession. Marshal Carver, Fire Chief Ormsby, and their several riders tagged along with the engine in scattered formation. Beside Ormsby, on the biggest and strongest horse they could find for him, Armand Sirois balanced his huge bulk in unfamiliar and precarious fashion, though it was Doc's guess he was enjoying the thrill of playing pioneer and riding in the great, open spaces of the American West.

The sun, having crossed the top of the clear sky long ago, was still adamantly blazing and hot; dust rose in the wakes of both vehicles as they jostled along the rutted highway. The riding horses Doc and Raider had brought for themselves, in the same boxcar that had transported Judith, the mule, were tied to the back of the wagon, where they followed without complaint.

"Wears me down, just ridin' like this," Raider said. "But come nightfall it's gonna be worth it."

"Yup," said Doc. "I expect it'll get cooler."

"That's not what I mean," said Raider.

"What do you mean?"

"I mean Claudette. She'll be sleepin' off by herself somewheres, and I mean to go callin'."

"How do you know she'll be by herself?"

"She'll see to it. I could tell by the way she looked at me before we left."

"Rade," said Doc, frowning, "far be it from me to interfere with your pleasures, but this time you might be taking too much of a chance. You and the little lady could get caught."

Raider shrugged. "I can take care o' myself, if we do."

"I know that. But there'll be a fuss. You'll turn the fat

Frenchman against you, and we might need him on our side. You never know. As for that gunslingin' marshal, well, you rubbed him the wrong way already. We ought to be thinking of some way to get back in his good graces.''

"What are we supposed to do—start kissin' his ass?''

"We don't have to go *that* far," Doc said dryly. "What I'm saying is if we're going to carry out an investigation in secret, we've got to look as innocent as can be, so we don't get any interference. In fact, that's why I suggested we go as veterinarians this time instead of medicine men. Too many of them have been just on the edge of the law, and folks these days are a lot more suspicious of purveyors of nostrums than they used to be.''

"Doc," said Raider, "you've got a way of makin' things more complicated than they are.''

"That's because," said Doc, "things have a way of being more complicated than they seem.''

They were silent for a spell after that, and there was only the creaking, jostling sound of the wagon, along with an occasional blowing grunt of mild protest from Judith, Doc's beloved mule, as she plodded forward. Doc jiggled the reins occasionally to let her know he expected a brisker pace, but all she did was turn her head, trying to look back at him in reproach.

"That there's one dumb mule," growled Raider.

"On the contrary," said Doc. "She doesn't stir herself a mite more than she has to. Knows how much she can get away with—exactly. Show me a horse that can cut it that fine.''

Raider snorted and said no more. It was an argument they'd never resolved, and probably never would.

The sun crossed the sky and began to lower itself in the west. They passed a colony of prairie dogs and looked at them without much interest. They saw a redtail hawk on a small, dead tree; it soared off, low, as they approached, and disappeared over a rise.

Raider let his head nod, closed his eyes, and dozed off

right where he sat, straight up on the wagon perch. Doc yawned. His own eyelids began to droop, and he caught himself and lifted his head again several times. Truth was, he needed sleep a lot more than Raider did. He'd put a lot of energy into the poetry lesson Virtue, with her long and sinuous limbs, had given him the night before.

Too bad, he told himself, he'd lost track of the number of times he'd managed to satisfy her, and himself along with it. Might be a record he could brag about. . . . Doc dozed off.

The sun was low and red in the west; dusk was only minutes away. The dirt road still stretched ahead of them, and Judith, her long ears twitching now and then, was still clopping along it at a slow walk. Without Doc awake to urge her on, she had slowed down to the pace she preferred—a speed you'd use to race a snail if you didn't care too much about winning. As Doc had dozed, the caravan ahead had pulled far out of sight and was somewhere beyond a low rise ahead—where suddenly the sounds of shots was coming from.

The sound brought both men awake in a fingersnap. Raider was fully awake; Doc was still coming up out of the molasses.

While Doc was still trying to unstick his eyes all the way, Raider leapt from his seat, ran to the back of the wagon, and, almost in one motion, untied his horse and sprang into its saddle. He was galloping hell-bent toward the low rise when Doc managed to leave the wagon seat and mount his own horse.

The rise was a rock-fault formation, and there was a jagged outcropping along its crest; Doc saw it as resembling the spine of an alligator, like the big ones you could find in the swamps of southern Georgia, though he expected Raider would have snorted at the comparison. At any rate, there was partial cover there, and by the time Doc reached Raider, he was already taking advantage of it. Dismounted, he was sprawled on a rock, leveling the

Model 94 Winchester 30-30 he kept scabbarded on his saddle as a matter of course, and obviously trying to get it fixed on a target somewhere below.

Doc sprang down from his own horse and skidded into place beside Raider.

Still peering along the sights of his repeating rifle, Raider said, "Shut up, Doc."

"I didn't say anything."

"Well, don't. I'm concentratin'."

Doc took in what he was concentrating upon. Six riders, most of them dismounted, had come upon the fire engine caravan ahead and below where the road crossed a broad hollow. The engine and the riders who had been escorting it were all halted. Guns were pointed at the marshal, Ab Ormsby, and the rest, and they all had their hands in the air. Two of the attackers were at the fire engine itself, one shoving a bundle about the size of a small valise under it.

"It's those hombres who stopped the train!" said Doc. "They're making a second try!"

"Shut up!" said Raider.

He scowled mightily along the sights of his weapon, getting his concentration back again. It was a good two hundred yards to the fire engine, and, although there wasn't any wind today, there was the elevation for that distance to be considered. Doc knew that any bullet traveled along a curve that was part of a parabola, and he'd tried to explain this to Raider on occasion, but Raider, who did it by feel, had always been impatient with such long-winded analyses.

Doc couldn't tell exactly what Raider had in mind for a target, but he could make a good guess. The rangy man he remembered as the apparent leader of the group was standing a stone's toss off from the fire engine, where he held both Carver and Ormsby in a frozen stance with their hands raised. He was profiled toward Raider and Doc, his revolver held out from his body and more or less silhouetted against the ochre dust.

Raider squeezed gently, and the Winchester barked loudly and jumped a little. The revolver flew from the rangy man's hand, which he immediately drew back and grabbed with a cry of pain. Everybody down there turned and looked up at the crest of the rise in amazement.

Raider lifted his head and bellowed, "Next one drops somebody!"

Doc wasn't sure they heard all his words clearly at that distance, but there was no doubt they got his meaning, more or less. The attackers hit the dust or scrambled for cover. Three of them ran immediately for their horses. You couldn't really call it cowardice; it just made good sense to scatter when somebody who was obviously a dead shot had the drop on you like that.

Raider put his next shot into the dirt near the feet of one of the horses, making it rear up and twist away in a frantic, sidestepping motion. That, as Raider might have said, and as he had undoubtedly meant it to do, put the lid on the jar. Stumbling wildly, all six men ran for their horses, leapt upon them, and rode off furiously in a scattered formation.

Raider rose. Doc looked at him thoughtfully. "How come you didn't drop one or two of 'em?"

Raider's glance said that right now Doc wasn't being as sharp as he always fancied himself to be. " 'Cause we don't know what's goin' on, that's why. We don't know yet who deserves to be dropped, and who don't."

Doc nodded. "Right. Exactly what I was thinking all along. Just a little surprised you saw it."

"Doc, how dumb do you think I am?"

"Oh, I don't know," said Doc. "About where the bird-lady in some freak show is? In the pointy-headed class, anyway."

"I'll settle your ass for that later," growled Raider. "Come on, let's get down there."

Everybody stared, pretty much in wonder, as Raider and Doc, mounted, trotted down to the group. Ab Ormsby stepped forward and was the first to speak. He ran his knuckle along under his chin whiskers. "Well, gents, looks like we're indebted to you again."

"*Oui, m'sieurs,*" said Sirois, waddling forward, rosebudding his lips as he spoke. "Your markmanship—it was *magnifique.*"

Dan Carver fixed his sour eye on Raider and made a kind of reluctant nod.

Raider nodded back to all of them and dismounted. He said to Carver, "Looks like you could have used our company after all, Marshal."

"Okay, Raider," said Carver, frowning. "I was wrong. Anybody can be, now and then. You want to ride along with us now, you're welcome."

"Of course!" Claudette piped up, her smiled turned unmistakably on Raider. "Most welcome!"

Carver swung a quick glance at the fire engine and the party's horses, a few of which had scattered themselves off a short distance. "Might as well make camp for the night now. You two can bring up that wagon of yours, if you want. We'll get a cookfire goin'."

"That mean we're invited to dinner?"

Carver shrugged. "Least we can do, I reckon." It struck Doc that his voice lacked the note of hospitality it ought to have had. His close-set eyes, which looked as though they'd been burned into his pockmarked face with a hot poker, still had a suspicious look to them as he held them on the two newcomers.

"Sounds fine," said Raider, nodding. "I expect we can talk while we eat. We got a few questions."

"Yeah," said the marshal, his eyes still firm on Raider. "So have I."

The campfire crackled away in its nest of little rocks, and the smell of coffee was fragrant in the cooling, darkening air of early evening. Saddles provided seats for everyone, and Armand Sirois, who had insisted on acting as cook, waddled back and forth, passing out the tin plates of salt pork and beans he'd heated up in a kettle over the fire.

"I must apologize!" he said, in that animated, over-expressive way of his, gesturing broadly with his free hand. "The food, it is not civilized! Without spices, without stock for sauce, I can do nothing!"

"Tastes okay to me," said Raider, mouthing a forkful.

Sirois shrugged. "At least it is not cooked to death. Beans must not remain too long on the fire. The sauce will lose all its flavor!"

"Whatever you say, mon-sewer," said Raider. He turned to Carver, as Sirois, having served everyone, lowered himself heavily upon a saddle to partake of his own fare. Raider turned to Ab Ormsby. "Well, Chief, I reckon it's time for me and doc here to get filled in on a thing or two. We been wonderin' about all kinds o' things. Like, how come a small town like Tamarack Springs orders this here fire engine all the way from France—must have cost a pretty penny. And how come them riders are tryin' to blow it all to hell?"

Ormsby set his plate down and took a corncob pipe from his pocket. "Mr. Raider, you got to understand, first, how things are up to the Springs, so I'll try to explain it. As I think you know, the town wasn't much originally, but got built where it is on account o' the springs in the nearby hills, which provide plenty of water. Back in the 'forties it was a rendezvous point for the fur trappers, like Taos and Jackson's Hole was. When the beaver was all trapped out, and when them silly-lookin' hats they made of it went out of fashion, the Springs started to attract others who might be wanderin' through these parts—explorers, buffalo hunters, a few homesteaders, and a passel o' just plain drifters. Wasn't many of 'em stayed on—most folks had their eye on California—on account of the soil wasn't the best for growin', though that was because nobody thought much to try irrigation in those days. And nobody realized back then that it was good cattle country, with plenty of open range like they got down Texas way. I'd say even better, on account o' the buffalo grass. Anyway, a few folks settled down and got the town started."

"Ab," said Carver sourly, "you gonna go on all night with this?"

"If need be," Ormsby said calmly. He had stuffed his pipe by now, and he paused to give it its first lighting. He took it from his mouth and blew smoke. "But Tamarack Springs was still a rendezvous point, only this time not for trappers. With crowds of folks comin' west like they were, and with railroads bein' built, it was just natural that a bunch o' coyotes would come along too, to take whatever they could get at gunpoint. After some gang pulled off a robbery somewhere and got wanted by the law, they found out Tamarack Springs, way off the beaten track, was a good place to go and hole up for a spell. And, without exactly sayin' it, they all sort of agreed not to pull no jobs in the Springs itself, and more or less behave themselves long as they were there. It was like goin' to a saloon and checkin' your guns at the door, if you see what I mean."

Claudette, listening intently, was wide-eyed. "I did not know this about your town, m'sieur. It is very exciting!"

Carver stirred and frowned at Claudette.

"Meantime," Ormsby continued, "a few ranches sprang up near the town, and that brought on some business in the town, like grain and feed, a livery stable, stores, and pretty soon a bank. Before you knew it, there was two main kinds o' folks in Tamarack Springs—those makin' their money from the visitin' outlaws, and those buildin' a regular cow town. The unofficial head o' the first group is Winfield Brent, who owns the Grand Palace. That's where all the shady characters head for when they blow in, and where Brent takes care of 'em, for a price. The rumor is, he even helps 'em plan jobs and find the kind o' men they're lookin' for—though nobody can prove that, for sure."

"Ab," interrupted Carver, "strikes me you're sayin' a little too much. I'll grant you these two gents helped us out some, but—no offense, gentlemen—we still don't know exactly who they are."

Ormsby looked at the marshal dryly. "I ain't tellin' 'em nothin' they can't find out for themselves pretty quick."

"That's right, Chief," said Raider. "Keep talkin'."

"Well, like I say, there's two groups. Brent and his folks, and the regular citizens, who are kinda led by Xavierina Larkin."

"By who?" asked Raider.

"Queersome name, ain't it?" said Ormsby, smiling. "You spell it with an X, though most of us just call her Rina, for short. She's been runnin' the XL ranch since her husband died, and doin' a damn good job of it. She pushes everybody into comin' to meetin's and makin' plans for the town. What they're really gettin' ready for is the spur the railroad's gonna build up from Yancy, on the main line. Once that's in, the cattle get loaded quick and easy, and there's enough profit to make it worthwhile raisin' them. Only trouble is, the bigger the town grows, the more respectable it gets. Schools, churches, that kinda thing. Which cuts into the town bein' a hideaway for outlaws, makin' business not so good for Brent and his followers. Last meetin' they had, there was a proposal to start allowin' extradition when lawmen come lookin' for somebody. Up to now, anybody who's wanted elsewhere gets protection, long as he's in the Springs."

"Ab," said Carver, "you're makin' it sound worse than it is. Any rough customer who blows in knows he's gotta behave himself while he stays at the Springs. He'll just get tossed out if he don't. What that amounts to is a real quiet town—we ain't had so much as a pocket picked for years. Even the cardsharps don't dare cheat nobody when they sit down to a game at the Grand Palace."

"That's right," Ormsby admitted. "You got an easy

job as marshal, and I can see why you're on Brent's side—I'm not pokin' at you, Dan, just statin' a fact. You got a right to your opinion. Even some of the regular citizens figger the way you do. But it all adds up to two groups against each other, and one o' these days they're gonna lock horns over it and have a showdown, which I ain't lookin' forward to with no amount o' pleasure. Most folks can't see it, but 'fore long we might have ourselves a regular little civil war in Tamarack Springs.''

Carver shook his head. ''You're blowin' it up too big, Ab. Won't ever come to that.''

''All this is mighty interesting,'' said Doc, chiming in, ''but it still doesn't explain the fire engine.''

Ormsby relighted his corncob. ''I reckon I'm to be blamed for that. When I heard the insurance rates'd go down if we had one I pushed hard and talked the town council into it. We'd already had three fires, and that helped. The insurance company's draggin' its ass payin' for those fires, but that's to be expected.''

''But how come you had this contraption sent all the way from France?''

'' 'Cause it's the best there is,'' Ormsby answered. ''That there newfangled pump Mon-sewer Sirois invented throws out water faster'n farther'n any other kind. I was a fireman back in Chicago in 'seventy-one. You know what happened there. Some folks say it was a cow kickin' over a coal-oil lamp, but that's a bunch of bushwah. It started in a lumberyard on the west side. More'n half the city went up in flames. Burned all night and all the next day. Over seventeen thousand buildings destroyed and at least two hundred and fifty people dead. Another hundred thousand homeless. It's somethin' I never hope to see again.''

He shuddered, puffed a little harder on his pipe, and stared off into the darkness beyond the campfire for a moment.

''Anyway,'' continued Ormsby, ''I stayed awake forty

hours helpin' to fight that fire. Breathed in so much smoke I got the lung trouble that brought me out here. I watched 'em try to fight that fire with piston and rotary pumps, and—excuse my French, ma'am—it was like tryin' to drown out Hell by pissin' on the edge of it. Yup, the monsewer's engine here, with the shippin' and all, may cost twice as much, but, like I finally convinced Rina, it's gonna be worth it."

"That there," said Carver sourly, "is *your* opinion. We'll see."

Doc nodded. "Well, now the only thing we don't know is why somebody doesn't want that engine to get to Tamarack Springs. Could that be this Brent feller you're talking about? To keep the town from growing?"

"Weatherbee," Carver said quickly, "I wouldn't make any accusations like that if I was you. If you're figgerin' on stayin' at the Springs, it wouldn't be smart at all to get Winfield Brent riled up at you."

"Just looking at possibilities," said Doc, shrugging. "No accusations. Not yet, anyway."

As Carver glared at Doc suspiciously, Raider rose and stretched himself. "Time to turn in, I expect. If we want a good early start in the mornin'."

"You have reason, m'sieur," said Sirois.

"Reason for what?" asked Raider, looking puzzled.

"It is the French way to say you are quite right," Claudette explained. *"Vous avez raison."*

Raider shrugged and wandered off toward the wagon, in which he and Doc would sleep for the night.

And now the moon was low in the west.

Raider and Claudette had found a perfect place of concealment among the jagged rocks atop the rise from which Raider's shots had driven off the attackers the previous evening. It was a sunken spot maybe the size of a small room, surrounded by sloping rocks that were about the height of a low fence. The ground inside was hard and sandy, but Claudette, slipping away from her snoring husband, had brought a blanket. She laid it out in the tiny depression. And then, quickly, she began to remove her clothes.

"Sugar," said Raider, also shucking his duds, "we better get right to it this time. If somebody at the camp sees you missin', they might come lookin' for us."

Naked, and on her back, so that her breasts were flattened a little by their own tremendous weight, Claudette brought her knees up as she spread her legs and, smiling, beckoned to Raider. "Put yourself into me, Raid-air, *mon cheri*," she said. "The old-fashioned way. It will be interesting, for a change."

He straddled her, supporting himself on his palms. He looked down into her round, bud-lipped face and saw her eyes begin to roll in anticipation of the ecstasy that would soon be upon her. She reached down, grabbed his gargantuan knob, and firmly steered it toward the pink, moist channel that bisected her thick patch of pubic hair.

Raider shoved. Hard. He went in to the hilt, and she cried aloud with both the pain and delight of it.

"Give it to me hard, Raid-air!" she breathed, closing her eyes and tossing her head from side to side. "As hard as you can!"

Raider started pumping with long, steady strokes.

He wasn't counting the strokes, but there must have been nine or ten before both of them suddenly heard the sound of voices. One was Carver's voice, evidently a short distance down the slope: "Maybe she's up there in them rocks!"

Ormsby's voice said, "Okay, let's take a look."

Raider withdrew and rose, his face twisted with anger. "Sonofabitch and goddamn!" he said. "Throw your clothes back on—quick! "

"*Merde!*" said Claudette, also scrambling to her feet.

"What's that mean?" asked Raider.

"Never mind—let us be quick."

Raider glanced across the rocks and down the slope, where the shadowed figures of Carver and Ormsby were already making their way toward them.

"I wonder," he growled, "if I'm *ever* gonna get to finish up with you proper."

CHAPTER FIVE

Ormsby had said that Tamarack Springs was divided in
two, as far as its citizens were concerned. The odd thing
about it, Doc reflected, after briefly sizing up his surroundings, was that it did seem to be two separate towns. The
straight main street ran roughly east and west, becoming at
each end a twisting, turning road that went toward some of
the ranches in the surrounding countryside. The center of
the town could be marked where the Grand Palace hotel
and saloon stood—a large, three-story frame building with
turrets, bay windows, and enough jigsawed foofooraw
along its eaves to make it look something like a miniature
castle. West of it was the barbershop, the livery stable, the
barn where cockfights were occasionally held, a small
stockyard, and, a respectable distance beyond all the main
buildings, the quiet-looking residence he guessed to be a
whorehouse. Having glimpsed the lacy underwear drying
on a line out back, he didn't have to guess very hard.

East of the saloon was the site of the town hall that had
burned down, the new firehouse, the bank, the general
store, and other establishments that were more or less
respectable. A short distance farther along, a number of
nicely built houses sat behind rows of elms and cottonwoods, now grown to maturity.

Raider and Doc were walking down this pleasant street

now, with Raider thinking it might well have been part of some settled town back in Arkansas, and Doc thinking the same thing, only about Pennsylvania.

"Big cream-color house, Ormsby said," muttered Raider. "Maybe that's it, way down at the end there."

"Looks like it might be," said Doc.

They quickened their pace a little.

Arriving with the others the previous evening, they had already taken Judith and their horses to the livery stable for a good currying, receiving permission to park the wagon there until they had use for it, and then they had supped at the Grand Palace, had a few drinks at the bar, and gone up to their double room for a good night's rest. Doc had soaked himself in the bath the hotel provided until Raider had hammered on the door to ask if he'd fallen in and drowned, and to remind him he wasn't the only one who wanted a bath.

When Raider had come back from his turn in the bath, he'd seen Doc bundled up in bed, perusing the town's weekly newspaper. "You gonna sleep already? Hell, I'm gonna get dressed and amble on down to that house where they're flyin' the lace underwear in back."

Doc frowned. "Rade, I know what's bustin' inside you, on account of that bad luck you've been having with Claudette. But patronizing the cathouse our first night here just might not be a good idea."

"Why the hell not?"

"Well, that sour-faced marshal and his pal, Winfield Brent, are still sizing us up. Carver's no doubt wondering how a vet's assistant learned to shoot the way you can, and suspecting you're not what you're pretending to be—which, of course, makes him dead right. As it stands, we're not sure yet just what role we're going to play—or exactly how we're going to play it. Might be we'll want to look real respectable, the way I do sometimes when I act as a traveling preacher. If you go see the ladies tonight, everybody's going to know it, and it might keep us from looking like real, upstanding citizens who figure on set-tling here.''

"Goddamn it, Doc!" said Raider, scowling deeply. "What am I supposed to do with these balls o' mine? They're ready to explode!"

"You might go back to that bath and take a real cold one this time," said Doc.

"Shee-it!" said Raider.

But he reached for his nightshirt instead of his clothes. Raider sometimes did see the good sense in Doc's asser-tions; he just hated to admit it, that was all.

They'd called on Ab Ormsby at the firehouse first thing in the morning, and it was he who had sent them to East Main Street to look for a big cream-colored house.

It came into sight fully now: A pleasant two-story clap-board structure with a broad front porch. A woman was in a rocker on the porch, shelling peas. Raider and Doc walked toward her, then came to a halt. Doc swept the derby from his head with a grand gesture, and Raider nodded, smiling almost pleasantly.

"Morning, ma'am," said Doc. "You must be Mrs. Ormsby."

She looked up. "Why, yes. And you must be the gen-tlemen who saved the fire engine. Ab told me all about it. Mr. Raider, and Doc Weatherbee, I believe."

"That's us, ma'am," said Doc. "And I expect Ab told you we were looking for a place to stay."

Ma Ormsby rose, shaking some of the pea shells out of her apron. She was a stocky woman with a clear complex-ion, and Doc guessed she must have been pretty and plump as a pigeon when she was younger. "We lost our one boarder just last week," she said. "He decided to go prospectin' up in Idaho. Nice young man. Of course, I wouldn't have had him here if he wasn't. Anyway, his room's empty and also the spare room, so you can both be private, if you want."

"Sounds like exactly what we want," said Doc.

"Room and board both is sixty dollars a month," she said. "I know that sounds high, but things are expensive here. Ab's pension don't go too far, and his new job as fire chief gives him more glory than it does wages."

"I reckon we can afford that much," grunted Raider. "Cheaper than that there hotel, anyway."

"You can look at the rooms if you like," she said.

"Lead the way, ma'am," said Raider.

The rooms, upstairs, were spic and span and nicely furnished. The beds, they discovered by pressing down on them, were satisfyingly soft. They tossed a coin for it, and Raider got the slightly larger room.

Ma Ormsby brought them downstairs again and into her huge kitchen in the back. She had an immense wood stove there that she must have brought with her from Chicago.

"Breakfast is at seven sharp," she said. "Dinner at six. Lunch is on your own, though I can pack one for you if you pay extra. Don't know if you heard or not, but I take a lot of pride in my cookin'. I used to cater for parties and such back in Chicago, and I still get called on occasionally here in the Springs." She laughed. "I reckon you'll both put on a pound or two if you stay here any time. I don't trust a man who's too thin. A little meat on the bones improves the disposition."

"That's what they say, ma'am," Doc commented politely. Truth was, he'd never really heard anybody say it.

"We'll go get our gear and move in," said Raider.

Ma Ormsby nodded. "If I'm not here, make yourself at home. There's a ladies' auxiliary meetin' at the church I got to go to. I take it both you boys are Christian gentlemen."

"I was once ordained a minister of the gospel, Mrs. Ormsby," Doc said suavely, "though I never practiced and decided instead to do the Lord's work by exemplary behavior wherever I found myself along life's great journey."

"Why, I'm glad to hear that," she said. "And you, Mr. Raider?"

"I'll be honest about my partner," Doc answered quickly. "He was once sunk in sin and degradation, but I showed him the error of his ways, and he is now completely reformed."

"Praise the Lord," said Ma Ormsby, beaming.

Raider glowered at Doc.

It took them perhaps an hour to bring their luggage from the hotel to the boarding house, which seemed empty when they returned to it. "Let's go down to the saloon and get the lay o' the land," said Raider. "We ain't run across this Brent hombre yet—he might be there now."

"Go ahead if you want," said Doc. "I gotta write up a report for the home office. You know how they are about weekly reports."

"To hell with 'em," Raider said. "Let 'em wait."

"No, let's keep 'em calm and happy, so they won't be pecking at us later, when we don't want it. I'll see you later."

Raider shrugged. "Suit yourself."

In a short time Doc was scribbling away at the small writing table in his room. The reports were the most annoying part of their jobs as Pinkerton operatives, and Doc took on the chore of writing them more or less by default. Old Allan Pinkerton, with his red squirrel-whiskers, probably would have gotten apoplexy over Raider's spelling and syntax.

He had finished two pages of what he figured would be three or four—the more long-winded they were the better the old man liked them—when suddenly, behind him, he heard the door to his room swing open.

He turned, supposing it would be Ma Ormsby, but it was not. A young woman stood in the doorway, staring at him. Doc rose from his chair, shuffling it aside.

"Mornin'," he said to the young woman.

"What in the name of the Devil's asshole," she said, "do you think you're doin' here?"

Doc's eyebrows rose. What she'd said, and the way

she'd said it, just didn't fit the face it had come out of. The girl was towheaded, fair-skinned, and buttermilk wholesome. She looked like somebody who'd be singing lead soprano in the choir of the church Ma Ormsby had gone to. Come to think of it, she favored Ma Ormsby slightly; her daughter, for a guess. She was just a tad plump, and would maybe fill in some when she got to be her mother's age, but right now it just meant that she showed a number of enticing curves, especially in the vicinity of her ample bosom. She wore a blouse that was threatening to fall off one pretty shoulder, and it was low enough to reveal the deep cleft between the tops of her breasts. At her waist, the blouse tucked itself into a tight pair of faded range jeans.

"Young lady," said Doc. "I might ask the same of you."

The girl had a second surprise for him. Without another word, she sprang forward, and, with the speed of a snake striking, grabbed his arm, twisted it, spun him around, and shoved it upward along his back in a painful hammerlock.

"Hey!" said Doc. "Now, goddamn it!"

He wouldn't have let a man do this to him, but the girl, with those big, innocent green eye of hers, and that little scattering of freckles across the bridge of her nose, had caught him completely off guard. He struggled to pull out of her grip, and she pushed his arm up hard so that the pain shot all the way from his shoulder to his elbow.

"You mangy sonofabitch," she breathed into his ear with that sweet voice of hers, "what are you after—money? We don't keep any in the house!"

"Now, hold on!" said Doc. "I'm Doc Weatherbee!"

"I don't care if you're James A. Garfield himself—you're not going to prowl around my house this way!"

"*Your* house?"

"Shut up! I'm taking your ass down to the marshal's office right now!"

Doc wrenched himself hard in another attempt to get out

of the hammerlock she'd twisted his arm into. Almost as though she'd been hoping he'd try that, she spun him around another way, and, as he swung off balance she ducked under him, put one arm between his legs and another behind his neck, then lifted him bodily from the floor, whirled him around twice, and sent him crashing down again, flat on his back, so that some of the breath was knocked out of him.

"Hey!" said Doc. "Take it easy!"

She came down upon him hard, and her knees slammed into his midsection, painfully racking away what little breath was left. The heel of her hand shoved his chin up and back so that his head struck the floor. Little flashing lights appeared for a moment before his eyes. She then slid one knee down between his legs and applied just enough pressure there to make him groan involuntarily.

"You make one more move, you bastard, and I'll crush your balls," she said. "If you've got any. Which I doubt."

It was probable, Doc was thinking, that if he fought back hard enough he could eventually subdue this girl. But the way she knew and used wrestling holds, there'd be a lot of fuss and considerable pain for both of them if he tried that. Words, he decided, were his best defensive weapon, under the circumstances. If she'd give him a chance to get them out.

Enough breath came back to him for him to gasp, "New . . . boarder . . . here . . . goddamn it! My room . . ."

He saw her expression change as she stared down at him, her big green eyes only inches away. With her bent over the way she was, he could see down the open front of her blouse, where her breasts hung, firm and bulbous. There was a pulse beat or two while the realization came to her. "Boarder?"

"Ma Ormsby just took us in. Me and my partner."

She stayed atop him, but took her hand away from his chin. "Why'n hell didn't you say so?"

"You didn't give me a chance. Who are you, anyway?"

"Heather Ormsby. She's my ma. What's your name again?"

"Weatherbee. Doc Weatherbee. My partner's name is Raider."

Heather cocked her head to one side. "You must be the two Pa was talking about last night. The ones that saved the fire engine."

"That's right. You gonna let me up now?"

An abrupt smile crossed Heather's face. "You really want to get up?"

It took him another moment to get her meaning—and even then he wasn't a hundred percent sure of it. "Well," he said, experimentally, "it's not *too* bad down here—long as you keep your knees to yourself."

Heather giggled. "I like rasslin'," she said. "How about you?"

"Depends on what kind," Doc said cautiously.

"There's not a boy in town I can't throw, if I've a mind to."

"I believe it," said Doc.

She now put her palm to his cheek, caressing it, getting the feel of it. She kept her eyes bright upon him. "Ma gets upset sometimes and says I'm too much of a tomboy. Pa doesn't mind, though. He wanted a boy, you see, and got me instead."

"Then he's got no cause to complain," said Doc.

"Doc Weatherbee, huh?" she said, still inspecting him closely. "Animal doctor, right? I think that's what Pa said. I like animals. Haven't found the bronc I couldn't ride yet. You know something? All the boys around here are scared of me."

"I can see where they would be," Doc said.

She had slipped her free hand down between his legs, and was massaging his crotch now. The soft lump she found there immediately began to harden, and, at that, her smile broadened a little. "Are *you* scared of me?"

"Well, not now," said Doc, grinning.

"You're better-looking than the boys around here," she said. "From the city, I'll bet. When I first saw you I thought you might be just a sissy."

"I've never been accused of that before," Doc said wryly.

"There's one thing, though," she said. "You don't know how to rassle worth a damn."

"Never got around to learning it, somehow," said Doc.

"Then maybe I better teach you some," said Heather.

"All right. One of these days I expect we can get around to it."

"Now," she said.

Doc eyebrows rose. "Now?"

"There's time. Ma won't get back for a couple of hours. I wouldn't be here myelf except I had to fetch some papers."

"What papers? You're way ahead of me."

"Town records. They ought to be at the town hall, but the town hall burned down, so I brought a bunch of 'em home."

"Do I take it you have something to do with the town records?"

"Hell, yes," said Heather. "I'm the town clerk. We're working in a back room of the bank till we get a new town hall built. But never mind all that. Let's do some rasslin'."

His thong had risen fully by now, and she was kneading it through his trousers, but still grinning at him as though to pretend she was hardly aware of what she was doing. "First thing," she said, "is that you can't rassle properly with your clothes on."

"Sounds logical," said Doc.

She lifted herself away from him at last, allowing him to pick himself up from the floor. She began immediately to strip her clothes away, glancing at him intermediately with a smile as she did so. Moments later they were both jaybird naked.

Casting his eyes appreciatively over her body, Doc

searched his mind for a word to describe it. Hefty? No—
she was a lot prettier than someone hefty would have been.
But the muscles of her arms and thighs were distinctly
marked, and obviously of considerable strength; they were
not concealed by flowing lines as such muscles are in most
women. Solid, that was it. Not hefty, but mighty solid.

She came toward him. "First, you grapple," she said.
"Like this."

She put her hands on his shoulders and, with her head
against his, arched her body back a bit, away from him.
Doc followed suit.

"And then, from the grapple position," said Heather,
"you go into a hold."

She swiftly thrust her arms under his shoulders and
brought her body forward, hard against him, pressing his
up-right member hard aginst his belly with her own belly,
wiggling a little to rub it as it stood there beginning to
throb. She hooked an ankle behind his heel and shoved
him backward over it, tripping him so that he fell on the
bed. As he fell, she stayed with him. And then, still
writhing, she twisted both of them around until he was on
top of her.

"Now, when I find myself like this," she said, looking
up at him, "it's a good time to switch right around—like
this."

She made the movement so quickly and deftly that he
wasn't sure just how she'd accomplished it. Before he
knew it, they were reversed, with Heather on top again,
and with her head down at his hips. Her own hips, and the
solid curve of her buttocks, floated just above his eyes,
and a thatch of moist blond hair peeked down at him, only
inches away. Below, he felt her mouth close upon his
knuckle, taking it deep. She bobbed her head up and
down slightly as she applied pressure with her lips and
sucked upon it. It was already hard, but he could feel it
swelling some more now, wanting to burst; her mouth was
as hot as the inside of a baked potato.

The pink crevice just above him was too inviting to ignore. He reached up, hooked his finger around the cheeks of her rump, and pulled the entire assembly down, crushing it into himself. His tongue flickered out until it found a tiny button. When the tip of his tongue touched it, he heard her moan with joy. She began to work her head up and down even faster, her lips still tight on the leathery cylinder of his penis. And now, stretching her legs out a little for support, she jammed her pelvis down upon him even harder, as though to smother him with that thick patch of hair and the soft, fleshy channel in the center of it. He shoved his lips to the button, sucked hard upon it, and at the same time worked his tongue back and forth across it.

She continued to moan through her tightened lips as her head went up and down, up and down, in ever faster strokes. Suddenly she opened her mouth and lifted it away. She did this only long enough to cry, "Come now, Doc! *With* me!" Then her lips closed over his rod again.

Doc let himself go. He heard her choking moan of delight as she swallowed his spurting juice. A great, tingling sensation, centered at his groin, spread like a prairie fire over the rest of him. Heather's pelvis jammed itself even harder into his face and he felt her shudder and throb with her own orgasm, working her strong thighs spasmodically against his cheeks, gripping his head as though to hold it there forever.

At last, when she'd sucked away every last ounce of his magic fluid, she rose away from his still throbbing cock and switched herself about so that they were head to head again. She rolled to her side, pulling him around to lie there, facing her. She smiled and ran her fingers lightly across his cheeks. "That was wonderful, Doc. You pack quite a load."

"A matter of diet," he said, smiling. "Eat all the prairie oysters you can get."

"I'll see that Ma lays some in," she said, laughing.

"Just give me about a minute," said Doc, "till it hardens up again, and then I'll put it where it belongs."

She shook her head abruptly. "I don't do it the regular way, Doc."

"You don't?" Doc wondered when this gal would run out of surprises.

"First—it's dangerous. That's how you make babies. Second—I'm saving it. For my husband, if I find him someday. It's only fair I have *something* new for him."

"Do you mean to say you, uh, never—"

"That's right," she answered. "Never did. The man who gets me gets a virgin."

"In a manner of speaking," said Doc, still amazed at her.

She dipped her head to one side and looked at him archly. "Disappointed?"

"Well, I was kinda hoping to finish this off right," he admitted.

"Forget that. We'll finish it my way. And if you're half the man I think you are, we've got a long way to go to the finish."

Before he could answer she was down upon his whip handle again, mouthing it gleefully, as it slowly swelled into hardness sufficient for a second round.

CHAPTER SIX

Raider half turned from the bar as Doc ambled toward him. His hand was on a shot glass of Millikan's Squirrel Whiskey he'd been nursing for the past twenty minutes. Ordinarily he would have been tossing down the stuff one shot after another, amazing Doc by never seeming to get fuzzy-headed with it, but today he was in one of the rare moods that sometimes came over him and dampened his interest in two-fisted drinking.

He looked at Doc and said, "Where the hell you been?"

"Writing that report." Doc bellied up to the bar and signaled to the bartender, who had bloodhound eyes with big pouches under them and who sported a pair of bright pink arm garters. "Beer with a shot o' whiskey in it," said Doc. "And add one raw egg, if you don't mind."

"One raw egg?" The drooping eyes opened a little wider.

"That's how I like it," said Doc. "Any objections?"

"Don't mean a rat's ass to me, mister," said the bartender, moving off.

Raider was still looking at Doc. "Writing that report, huh?"

"That's what I said."

"Well, you're lyin', Doc. One, it don't take this long to write one report, not even for the old buzzard we work for.

Two, you only order that raw egg in your beer—which is enough to make a man puke—when you been gettin' off your rocks too many times. So tell me the truth. Who was she?''

Doc sighed. ''Ma Ormsby's got a daughter who likes to rassle. But never mind that for now. What have you been finding out here in the Grand Palace?''

Raider swung a slow glance around the big room. Beyond the bar were tables at which men were sitting—drinking, talking, some toward the rear playing poker. At the far end of the room was a small stage with a piano beside it, unoccupied at the moment. ''Mainly, I've been finding out that Tamarack Springs is still a hideaway, just like it always was.''

''That so?'' Doc inspected the room for himself.

''Look close at a few of 'em,'' said Raider. ''That quiet shorty feller over there who looks like a White Cherokee. Luke Hamlin—used to ride with the Allisons. Over on the wall, playin' cards—the one with the black hat—that's Curley Loudermilk, who's robbed more trains than they can put in a railyard. There's others, but you can spot 'em as well as I can, I reckon. Rewards out on every one of 'em. A bounty hunter could make himself a millionaire here—if he dared try.''

The bartender returned with doc's concoction; Doc put a coin on the bar and glared at the man to keep him from commenting. The bartender shrugged and moved off again.

''So it looks like this Winfield Brent is still doing pretty good business. Seen him yet?''

Raider glanced at the encased pendulum clock on the wall behind the bar. ''Supposed to be he gets here any minute now. Nobody looked suspicious when I asked for him. Seems like that's what anybody new in town always does. Checks with him first.''

Doc frowned. ''I wish we'd known all this when we set up the operation. Might've been better if we pretended to be on the owl hoot ourselves. Though I suppose that would've meant paying Brent his fee, and you know how the office is about extra expenses.''

"What *do* we tell this hombre Brent when we see him, anyway?''

"What we've been telling everybody," said Doc, shrugging. "That we mean to open a veterinary practice here; that we've got a wagon to take us out to the ranches for castrating and one thing and another—hope I still have those Burdizzo forceps, practically no bleeding when you use 'em.''

"You sure talk like you know what you're doin', Doc,'' said Raider, squinting at him. "I just hope you really do.''

"I always know what I'm doing,'' Doc said smugly. "And that reminds me, when we see Brent, for Christ's sake, let *me* do the talking.''

"That won't be hard,'' said Raider. "Once you get started, nobody else can get a word in.''

"Rade,'' said Doc, "you're carryin' a big grouch these days. Maybe you *better* find yourself a woman. Where's the French gal?''

"Damned if I know,'' said Raider, frowning. "Wasn't in her room. Maybe she's down at the firehouse with her husband. I understand he and Ormsby are gettin' the new fire engine ready.''

"Well, if she wants to finish up what you two started as much as you do, she'll find a way. So be patient.''

"*I'm* patient,'' growled Raider. "It's my cock that's chafin' at the bit.''

There was a stirring at the front door. Raider and Doc turned to look and saw a tall man in a dark coat and a brocaded vest enter. He strode into the place with a confident air of ownership, and they knew at once that this was Winfield Brent.

A step behind him, on one side, was a man whose nationality they couldn't place immediately; you saw everything from Irish immigrants to Chinese laborers in the West these days, but he was neither of these. He was immense, with bare arms the size of most men's thighs showing from a vestlike garment he wore over an otherwise bare torso. His head was as bald as a bowling ball, the skin on it a deep mahogany tan. Mustaches swept out like scimitars from under his mashed lump of a nose. He was fat—very fat—but it was obvious that there were strong muscles under those layers of fat.

Brent's other companion, also a step behind him, was Marshal Dan Carver, whom they'd already met. Carver, with his nicked-hatchet profile, looked like some predator, alert and prowling for game.

Brent, his eyes firmly on Raider and Doc, walked directly toward them. He was well groomed, Doc saw; the silvery, close-cropped mustache just above his thin, chiseled lips gave him a certain handsome and even aristocratic look. He aimed his eyes at the two newcomers like a pair of blued gun barrels. He halted, and Carver and the huge bald man halted behind him. He held his aim for a moment before he spoke.

"Evenin', gentlemen," he said softly, in a strong and pleasant voice. "I don't believe I've had the pleasure of meetin' you before. My name is Brent; Winfield Brent. I understand you've already met Marshal Carver, and my other associate here has a name that even I can't pronounce, so we all just call him Turk."

The South was in his voice; the deepest part of it, where Spanish moss hangs on cypress trees. The South and all its grand old courtesy. But his hard eyes didn't match it.

"Brent, huh?" said Raider. "We heard about you."

Doc nudged him to remind him that he wasn't supposed to do the talking. "Fine place you've got here, Mr. Brent," said Doc, his air almost as courtly as Brent's. "We didn't expect to find anything so elegant out here off the beaten track."

"I'm pleased you find it to your likin', gentlemen." Brent dipped his head in the suggestion of a bow. "I've heard you intend to establish a veterinary practice here."

"That's right," said Doc. "We heard it's needed."

"No doubt," said Brent. "But I've also been wonderin' if treatin' sick animals is all you have in mind to do."

"What else would we be doing?" Doc was all innocence.

"I don't know exactly," said Brent, holding his smile. "It just occurred to me that a couple of gentlemen as familiar with firearms and as fearless in the face of attack as I've heard you are might have somethin' else in mind."

Doc shrugged. "Traveling around like we do, we learn to take care of ourselves. We've had to trade lead with a few misguided hombres now and then, but it's not what we prefer. That's why we're ready to settle down if we can find the right place. Tamarack Springs might be it."

"I see." Brent nodded. "Now, I'm not doubting your word, gentlemen, or prying into your histories, which would not be at all courteous. But it might be well to remind you that anyone who's had—uh—certain misunderstandings with the authorities elsewhere usually consults me about his problems when he arrives. There are certain arrangements to be made for the benefit of our community and of anyone who stays here a spell. Occasionally a newcomer who has such problems neglects makin' these arrangements. In such a case, he leaves here rather quickly, and sometimes not on his own two feet."

Raider glared at the hotel owner. "Is that there some kind o' threat?"

"Why, certainly not, sir," said Brent suavely. "I am merely tryin' to acquaint you gentlemen with the customs of our community. In fact, I'll be pleased to consult with you further on the matter in private. Shall we say by tomorrow evenin'? That should give you time to decide whether or not you really want to stay here."

"Maybe we'll drop around," said Raider. "Maybe not."

"Mr. Raider means," Doc said quickly, "that we will give full consideration to your kind invitation."

"Good." Brent nodded. "Meanwhile, gentlemen, enjoy yourselves. The next round of drinks is on the house."

When Brent had stalked off, Carver and Turk still in his wake, Raider watched him disappear through a door in the back of the room, then turned to Doc and said, "God-damn! I never heard so much polite talk that wasn't really polite all in one piece!"

"That's his style," said Doc with a shrug. "Best way to handle it is to go along with it. And don't let down your guard."

"What in hell are we foolin' around with him for, anyway?"

"We don't seem to have a choice, Rade. He's the one who opened fire, not us. If we're going to stay here and do our job, we'll just have to figure a way to deal with him."

Raider downed what was left of his Millikan's Squirrel Whiskey but made no move to signal the bartender for another. "I'd feel better about everything," he said, "if I could just find me a quick piece of ass somewhere. What about this gal back at the boardinghouse?"

"Heather?" Doc smiled. "You know the rules. The gals belong to whoever gets 'em first, so she's mine."

"Who said that was a *rule*?"

"You did, Rade. First time we had a fight over it. So don't try to change it now."

"Shee-it!" Raider said in disgust.

"Come on," said Doc. "Let's get back. Ma Ormsby expects us to be on time for meals—and I hope her cook-ing's as good as she says. I used up a lot of energy today, and I'm hungry."

CHAPTER SEVEN

Ma Ormsby had not exaggerated. The table where they ate was in the huge kitchen rather than in a separate dining room, and upon it Ma laid out what Raider and Doc could only think of as a sumptuous feast, though they gathered that, for the Ormsbys, this was merely daily fare.

The Yankee pot roast was rich, brown, and tender, with chunky potatoes, carrots, and onions a part of its sauce, and on the side were the peas she'd been shelling earlier, in a creamy sauce that had an elusive, tart flavor—a touch of wine, Doc guessed. There was a whole loaf of hot, fresh-baked bread and a crockpot of pale gold, freshly churned butter. The jam was maypaw, which Doc had had before in Louisiana; someone had evidently planted the right kind of hawthorn bushes in the vicinity of Tamarack Springs.

Ma beamed happily at their compliments, which they meant with all their hearts.

Heather Ormsby sat in her place across from Doc, shooting sly smiles in his direction now and then. She paid hardly any attention at all to Raider, which made him scowl even more deeply.

Ab Ormsby, having returned from his day's chores at the firehouse, was in his new fire chief's uniform. It wasn't exactly new, they learned from the conversation, but his old lieutenant's uniform from the Chicago Fire Brigade, let out considerably and resewn by Ma, with a lot more gold braid she'd found somewhere tacked onto it. He'd removed the jacket to come to the table, where he sat in a snowy white shirt and broad, bright red suspenders.

Ab had tied a napkin around his neck, and he kept using the edge of it to wipe gravy from his Lincoln-style chin whiskers. "Good food, clean, high air," he said. 'Ain't nothin' like it for a man. After I swallered all that smoke in Chicago the doctors sent me out here with a year to live. That was almost ten years ago, and I'm still kickin'—stronger'n ever. Doctors don't know their butts from a hole in the ground. Don't mean you, Weatherbee—no offense."

"None taken," said Doc. "How's the new fire engine?"

"Well," said Ormsby, leaning back in his chair, "we got a problem or two, I'm afraid. There's a lot of it that still ain't put together—pipes and valves and things. Good thing Monsewer Sirois come along with it. He's got all these drawings I can't make head nor tail out of. It'll be a few days, I expect, before we get her workin'. We'll just have to take a chance we don't get another fire before she's ready."

Doc looked up curiously. "Sounds like you're expecting another fire, Ab," he said.

Ormsby frowned slightly. "I ain't sayin' I am, and I ain't sayin' I ain't."

"That means you *are* sayin' it. But it's dangerous to say. Is that it?"

"Now, don't go twistin' me around here," said Ormsby, reaching forward to spear another potato for himself. "It's just that we had more'n one fire lately, with more'n one building burning down at a time. When there's a wind, anything nearby catches fire too. That's how we lost the town hall, when a carpenter shop almost next to it busted into flame one night. The carpenter had to go out of business and leave town."

"Wait a minute," said Doc. "If he was insured, how come he had to go out of business?"

"Couldn't wait to get the claim paid. You see, the way it works is the town insures all commercial establishments in the city limits, takin' advantage of the group policy they can get. Most of the merchants couldn't afford individual policies. But the town can't pay off till the insurance company does—there just ain't that much money in the treasury. Takes months to get the claim settled, which we didn't know when we signed up for the scheme. Some folks, like that carpenter, just can't hold out that long and they have to sell out. The bank ain't so sure they'll ever get their money, so they won't make no loans. As a matter of fact, if any of these fires was arson, there ain't never gonna be a payoff."

"And you suspect arson?"

"If I did," Ormsby said soberly, "I might be keepin' some folks from ever makin' good on their losses. The other thing is, just suspectin' arson and provin' it are two different things. That's why I ain't made too much fuss over what I saw. It just wouldn't get nobody nowhere."

"Just what did you see, Ab?" Doc asked casually.

Ormsby frowned. "This here's a sleepin' dog that better keep on sleepin' awhile. Ma, whatta you got for dessert tonight?"

There was ragged cloud cover that night and a wind to blow it eastward, toward the mountains. The moon was shuttered by shreds of passing cloud, so that one minute there was light, and the next there was not. Raider held up a coal-oil lantern, which he'd fetched from the wagon, while Doc looked at the charred timbers where the carpenter shop had been. The site was off the main street, toward the creek that ran past the town, and from here they could see some of the lights glowing in the Grand Palace saloon and just barely detect some of the faint sounds of revelry issuing from it.

"Doc," said Raider, "let's knock it off. Nothin' here but a lotta charcoal."

Doc frowned stubbornly. "If Ab Ormsby saw something here, we can see it too."

"Not the way he can. He knows all about fires. We don't."

"If there's some kind of evidence," persisted Doc, "it only takes common sense to see it. Just hold that lantern and be patient, all right?"

"The night ain't gettin' any younger," said Raider. "I was figuring' on wanderin' down to the hotel. Claudette might just be findin' some way to duck out on that fat husband of hers, and if she does she'll be lookin' for me."

"You can go snoopin' around for her all you want, as soon as we finish here. Just give me a few more minutes." Doc lifted a blackened beam and moved it to one side. Most of the upper part of the structure had burned, and what had been its four walls now formed a kind of jagged fence with numerous gaps in it. The floor itself had not burned as much as the upper parts had in the rising flames, and portions of the inner walls were still standing.

"Let me ask you somethin', Doc," said Raider. "Suppose you find this here fire was set, like Ab said it was. What the hell good is that gonna do us?"

"The insurance company'll be happy to hear it. That'll make the old man happy, and he might even come up with a bonus for us. Allan Pinkerton may be a penny-pinchin' Scotchman, but he does cough up a little extra for us now and then when he likes what we've done. I guess he figures it'll keep us from quitting, like we threaten all the time."

"If I don't get me a piece of ass pretty soon," grumbled Raider, "I really will quit. And both you and old Allan can buy a ticket to Hell, for all I care."

"Wait a minute," said Doc. "Look at this." The circle of light from the lantern was on a charred spot on the floor against part of a wall that was still standing. Leaning over,

Doc traced the discoloration with his hand, showing how it seemed to climb the wall before it disappeared. His eyes darted about in the rubble to one side of that area, and suddenly he bent forward and picked up an object he'd spotted. He moved it under the lantern. "What's this look like to you?"

"Part of a cider jug. Why?"

Doc sniffed the large shard, then handed it to Raider. "Smell it, Rade. It wasn't cider in that jug; it was coal oil. What's that fancy name they give it sometimes? Kerosene."

Raider brought the clay piece to his nose. "Damned if you ain't right, Doc. Looks like somebody *did* start this fire. But we still don't know what for. And, to tell you the truth, I ain't even sure I give a damn what for."

There was the sound of a shot.

Almost simultaneously a slug struck the remains of the wall near where they stood, sending splinters flying. Raider immediately blew out the lantern, set it down, snaked his .44 out of its holster, and put himself into a crouch, accomplishing all of this in a continuous motion and in not much more than two seconds. Doc, his own Diamondback drawn, hunkered down beside him. Both men peered at the darkened field beyond the ruins of the town hall.

"See anything?" whispered Doc.

"Shut up," said Raider. "Gimme time to get my owl eyes."

Doc, too, waited for the moments to pass so that his own vision would adjust to the darkness. Out there in the field there were only the vague shapes of old fence posts and a line of red willows along a creek that ran past the outer edge of the town. Once, Doc thought he detected shadowed movement near the creek, but in the next instant he was ready to admit it might have been his imagination. "Sounded like maybe a rifle," he whispered.

Raider nodded. "It must've come from near the creek. That's the only real cover out there. Hold on. I just saw somethin' move."

"Well, give it a blast. You're the sharpshooter."

"A hand iron won't do it this far," said Raider, shaking his head. "Doc, light that lantern again."

"Light the lantern? Have you gone loco?"

"Turn the wick down and keep it low. Set it somewheres so's he can see it, then reach out and move it every once in a while."

"And draw his fire on *me*? Like hell, Rade."

"Listen to me, goddamn it," Raider said. "He'll see that light and figure we're both still here. Only I'm gonna be circlin' around him and get the drop on him."

"Yeah, while he's shootin' at *me*."

"You been shot at before, ain't you?"

"I never said I liked it."

"Do like I say, damn it! It's the only way we can get him."

Doc, scowling mightily, saw Raider's point, though he hated to own up to that. "Go on," he growled. "I'll keep his attention."

As Raider moved off in a crouch, Doc took the lantern to a spot behind a jagged portion of the outer wall, found a match, lighted it once more, and turned the knob to lower the wick. He then raised it over his head so that it would be visible out there in the field.

Almost immediately there was a second shot. Doc heard the bullet strike the outer wall—much too close to where he was for him to feel easy about it. His lips moved as he muttered to himself almost inaudibly. "This," he said to nobody in particular—since nobody in particular was near— "is a hell of a way to spend the evening."

Raider was already out in the field, some distance to the right of the charred ruins, running in a bent-over position seeking slight hollows wherever he could find them, and taking care not to move noisily through any brush or stumble on rocks or ruts in the earth. He made his progress in a series of brief dashes, freezing still whenever the moonlight came momentarily through a break in the clouds, running whenever it darkened again.

Twice he heard shots from the willows along the creek as Doc exposed the lantern. The second time he saw the muzzle flash: A bright orange scratch on the surface of the darkness.

Moments later he came to the creek, at a point perhaps a hundred yards upstream from the willow clump. He jumped across the narrow stream and scrambled up on its opposite bank. Then, still in a crouch, and moving cautiously with toed-in steps, he started toward the willows.

The darkness he was peering into now seemed to deepen. He glanced at the sky. A bigger cloud was covering the moon, and it looked as though it was going to be there for a while.

Scuffling sounds came to his ears from the vicinity of the willows, and he squinted harder, trying to detect movement. He thought he saw a shadow shift itself, there in the willows; he thought, as he tried to focus on the distance, that it began to take on form—the shape of a man hunkering down to fire a rifle. He wasn't a hundred percent sure of this—it could be branches, or a rock, or a stump—but he knew the outlines of what he saw would become clearer as soon as that extra-big cloud up there got out of the moon's way. Moving with utmost care, he took another step forward.

There was a whirring, stuttering sound at his feet. He was startled as what seemed to be a couple of small bundles rose from the grass and hurtled away from him, curving up into the air. The beating of their wings was like soft drumming on a Cheyenne tom-tom.

Ahead, where he'd thought he'd seen a shape, there was a scuffling sound and a snapping of underbrush. Whoever was there had heard the damn quail birds Raider had flushed clearly enough—and, of course, had guessed immediately that someone was stalking him. He fired at what appeared to be a bulky, moving shadow scuttling away from the creek. It was still hard to know exactly what he was seeing, but his impression now was that the shadow kept moving, unhit by the slug he'd sent its way. A moment later he heard the sound of horse's hooves, and a moment after that the moon peeked down on the field again. He could now make out the silhouette of a horse and rider rapidly disappearing over a rolling crest of land; he lifted his .44 for another shot, but even before he got his eye on the sights, he knew his target was much too far. He fired anyway. Orange flame spurted from his weapon as it bucked in his hand. He blinked. The horse and rider were gone.

Raider blew on the muzzle of his revolver, then holstered it again. He stared at the crest where the rider had disappeared, and said softly to himself, "Sonofabitch." Then he turned back toward the charred remains of the building and called out to Doc, to keep from getting shot at by his own partner.

Moments later he was explaining to Doc what had happened. "Damn birds!" he said. "Next time I see a quail, I'm gonna blow the little fucker's head off."

"Oh, I expect you'll have cooled down by then," said Doc. "What I'm still wondering is who was trying to dry-gulch us and why?"

"Somebody who didn't want us pokin' around in these ashes—that's for sure."

"Which means somebody here has an idea we're not exactly who we say we are. That could mean either the marshal or Mr. Fancy-Pants Brent—they've already said as much."

Raider shrugged. "Stewin' on it ain't gonna get us anywhere. We just have to wait till somebody shows his hand. As for me, I've had enough pussyfootin' around for one night. I don't know about you, but I'm goin' to the hotel and find out where that little French gal is."

"All right," said Doc. "You go ahead. I'm going back to the boardinghouse."

"Which means," said Raider, grinning, "that you got the same thing on your mind I have."

"Good hunting," said Doc with a laugh.

"Same to you, partner," Raider said.

The clouds were thinning out now, with only torn streaks crossing the moon, which was hurrying westward as though to crawl down below the horizon there and rest a spell. The stars were beginning to show again, like the burning, phantom eyes of ten thousand deer in a thicket, watching the ghosts of the old mountain men go by: Jim Bridger, Bill Williams, Long Hatcher, Kit Carson, and the others who'd been the first—but for the Indians—to come this way. Maybe they knew that someday the towns would spring up here. Maybe they knew that some of them would start to grow. Maybe they knew there'd be growing pains.

Raider ran his palm gently over Claudette Sirois's magnificent rump. He was on his knees on the bed, and she was on her hands and knees before him. *"A la chien!"* she had said. "As the dogs do, that is what I wish. And deeply, Raid-air, as deeply as you can with that great stick of yours!"

Arriving at the hotel, he'd found Claudette and her husband in the dining room, which was separate from the saloon, having a late supper. He'd made small talk with both for a moment, excused himself, taken a room from the desk clerk, then returned and casually worked his room number into the conversation. Claudette heard it, smiled, and nodded. Armand kept on talking about the abominable, uncivilized food to be found in these parts.

Two hours later Claudette was knocking softly on his door. He let her in, and they were both so eager that they began to strip themselves immediately.

And now the preliminaries Claudette insisted upon had been taken care of, with Raider astonished that he was able to hold himself in, and she was ready to let him reach his own bursting release. The tip of his cudgel eased its way into her soft folds as she reached back to guide it. He held her firmly by the sides of her buttocks and paused before thrusting, flexing and readying the muscles of his thighs.

"Now!" she said.

He slammed his hips forward, and his great member sank into her for its full length.

Her gasping cry of delight was very close to a scream. She was already jerking spasmodically with the first of the many orgasms she would enjoy as Raider, working his piston back and forth, pumped himself into her. He felt his own climax rising within him at last. He tried to hold it back a little longer but there was too much of it, and it exploded out of him like horses leaping from a burning barn. She shuddered and laughed and wept and cried out, "More, more, more!"

At that moment, Doc was in bed too—his own, at the boardinghouse. He lay on his back, his hands folded behind his head, and looked down at the golden mop of Heather's hair as she mouthed his stubby rod, alternately sucking at the head and running her lips up and down the stem of it. He had almost fallen asleep when she'd tiptoed into his room, put a finger to her lips to warn him into silence, then slipped into the bed with him. That had been more than an hour ago, and in that time she had all but exhausted him.

"Tell me something," he said to the bouncing towhead down there. "Just how long can you keep this up, anyway?"

"As long as you can, Doc," she said, looking up, laughing. "And maybe longer."

Doc sighed. His eyelids fluttered down, fluttered up, then fluttered down again. He nodded, jerked his head upright, and then it fell again. A warm gray curtain of sleep began to close over his mind. He tried to hold it back at first, and then what was like his own voice, deep and distant inside of him somewhere, said, "To hell with it." He let the curtain shut itself all the way.

Moments later Doc began to snore softly.

Heather looked at him, showing at first an expression of mild surprise, and then she laughed abruptly. She returned to his still upright bludgeon, closed her lips over it again, curled herself into a comfortable position, and, with her pacifier in place, closed her own eyes and began to sleep along with him.

CHAPTER EIGHT

It was partly the need to sit back, sum things up, and decide how to proceed next that brought Doc and Raider into the Grand Palace saloon about midday of the following day. That and the ice cold beer they'd heard about. It seemed that on the train that brought the fire engine there had also been a shipment of beer-cooling equipment Brent had purchased for his establishment, made by the Finstetter Brothers in Allentown, Pennsylvania, where the descendants of King George III's Hessian mercenaries knew a great deal about beer and how it should be served. It was a newfangled idea that interested Doc—instead of trying to ice the kegs, you ran the beer through copper coils encased in ice and that way it became much more deliciously cold. Ice, brought down from the hills in winter and stored in a half-buried icehouse, was available in Tamarack Springs, though at two cents a pound most people considered it an expensive luxury.

For a degree of privacy, Raider and Doc chose a table in a far corner of the room, behind a huge rubber plant in a shiny green pot. They had spent the morning readying the wagon for its veterinary service, unlashing equipment and supplies that had been made for the journey, and washing down the vehicle so that its gaudy paint glistened like new. Neither had commented to the other upon their romantic activities of the previous night. A few side glances between them were enough to communicate, in general fashion, what had transpired.

Raider drank his beer through the cream foam and smacked his lips. "Not bad." That was his way of saying damn good.

"I agree," said Doc, nodding. "Brent's made quite a showplace of this saloon, way out here past hell and gone. Must be he realizes a handsome profit from the shady characters that come here to hole up for a while. That little gal, Heather, knows a lot about what's going on in town, and she's been able to fill me in. Brent owns the hotel, the saloon, and the whorehouse. The outlaws are required to pay him a fee when they blow in, like it was room and board, only one hell of a lot more expensive. That way, they're guaranteed they won't be extradited if the law comes looking for them, and that any bounty hunters who show up will be discouraged, usually with a few ounces of lead. Most of them blow in with loot on them, so Brent gets not only their fee but what they spend on entertainment. Heather says sometimes they blow their whole roll before they leave. Easy come, easy go. A lot of these boys are that way."

"And if the town gets too respectable," said Raider, "Brent stands to lose all that. Which means he could have had those fires set just so that Larkin woman and her crowd wouldn't get too far with their plans to build up the town. He also could have sent those masked coyotes after the fire engine. With Marshal Dan Carver in cahoots—just pretendin' to put up a defense. That would explain why Carver didn't want us taggin' along in the first place."

"Of course, we don't have much proof of any of this," said Doc, "and that's what we've got to get next. We're gonna need some time. I think we ought to telegraph Denver, tell them what little we know, and advise them we're sticking around awhile."

"Which means ridin' down to Yancy, where the telegraph line is. You're goin' by yourself this time, Doc. I'm not comin' along just to shinny up that pole and hook in your equipment for you.''

"Nobody asked you to," said Doc.

Raider narrowed one eye suspiciously. "Wait a minute. I know why you want to take the trouble to ride all the way back to Yancy. That skinny redhead who spouts poetry."

"That's right, come to think of it. I almost forgot about her."

"The hell you did. You'd cross Donner Pass in the dead of winter if you thought there was a free piece of ass on the other side of it."

"Drink your damn beer, Rade," said Doc. "Just shut up and let me sit here and think a spell."

As Doc sat back, meditating, the sound of voices came to him from the other side of the rubber plant. He heard a man say, in what sounded faintly like some kind of foreign accent, "So now you're in a very bad position, already. My bishop's got your knight pinned. The same move the the great Morphy defeated the Duke of Brunswick with in Paris, way back in 'fifty-eight."

"You think you've got me, huh, Sam?" said the other man's voice. "Well, you've got another think coming. My rook goes here—and it's check. Now, let me see you get out of that one."

Doc's expression brightened. He'd tried to teach Raider chess, but Raider had been bored with it. Poker and black-jack were more to his liking, especially if high stakes were involved. Doc rose, circled the rubber plant, and came to the table behind it, where the two men he'd heard had set up a board with wooden chessmen on it.

The smaller of the two looked up at Doc. He was dark and wiry and his eyes were bright and restless; Doc thought he detected a faint glint of mockery in them, as though this man found the world absurd and had decided to laugh at it instead of worry about it. He wore a dark and rather formal suit, but he had not bothered to put a collar on his shirt. He stared at Doc defensively for a moment, then said, "So we're playing chess. Some reason we shouldn't, already?"

"Every reason in the world you should," said Doc. "You mentioned Paul Morphy a moment ago. A great genius. Did you know he was already defeating the best players in New Orleans at the age of twelve?"

The little man broke into a broad smile. "Sit down, sir!" he said. "Watch me give my friend Uriah here a chess lesson!"

Doc returned the smile and shuffled out a chair for himself. "I'm Doc Weatherbee, practical veterinarian," he said.

"We are pleased to make your acquaintance," said the little man. "My name is Ruby—Sam Ruby—and I make the finest jewelry anywhere west of New York." He nodded to his companion. "This is Mr. Uriah Van Hawley, the noted historian."

Uriah Van Hawley was a bulky man with a full beard that came down to the middle of his chest. He looked more like a miner than a historian. He had bright blue eyes that seemed to lurk with a certain amount of caution in their little caves under his immensely bushy eyebrows. He inspected Doc carefully for a moment, then said, "Sam exaggerates. I may be something of a historian, but I'm not exactly noted. Anyway, watch me give him a good drubbing."

Doc watched, slowly sipping the beer he had brought with him. Several times each man glanced up at him before moving, as though seeking approval or disapproval, but he kept his face expressionless. Advising a chess player could be dangerous—especially if it turned out to be the wrong advice.

Eight moves later, it was all over. Sam Ruby wriggled out of check, made a brilliant sacrifice of his knight, and then suddenly, with a series of moves Doc hadn't foreseen, drove Van Hawley's king to the edge of the board and checkmated him there.

"Very nice," said Doc.

"He got lucky," Uriah grumbled.

Sam looked at Doc. "You'd like maybe to take on the winner?"

"You two go ahead," said Doc. "I got too much on my mind today to concentrate."

They were setting up the chessmen again when the bartender with the sad, bloodhound's eyes came up to the table. He polished a glass with his apron as he stood there glaring down at Sam and Uriah. "You two in here again usin' up a table?"

Uriah drew himself up. "It's a public place, isn't it?"

"Not to you two, who never order a drink, it ain't. I told you before. The tables are for payin' customers, not deadbeats. You gonna skedaddle, or do I call the bouncer?"

"Just a moment," said Doc. "These two gentlemen are my guests. I'd take it kindly, bartender, if you'd bring them both a beer."

The bartender scowled, looked for a moment as though he might say something, then evidently changed his mind and moved off.

"Very good of you, sir," Sam said to Doc. "We would like to reciprocate, but we are temporarily without funds."

"Temporarily, hell," grumbled Uriah Van Hawley, leaning back and smoothing down his beard. "You might as well know, Weatherbee; we are permanently and chronically without funds, both Sam and myself. Nobody buys his damn jewelry, not with the Navaho stuff they can get in these parts, and there surer'n hell isn't a market for what *I* do in Tamarack Springs."

"You mean writing history?"

"Exactly," said Uriah, nodding gravely, and compressing the great, woolly beard that hung from his chin like a knitted bib. "*The Outlaws of the Frontier*. I've been working on it for years. Someday every scholar in the world will turn to it as the definitive account of what really happened out here.''

Sam shrugged. ''So he says, over and over again. Sits in that cabin of his and writes away. But nobody ever sees what he writes.''

''It will be seen,'' said Uriah, ''when it's finished.''

At this point the bartender returned and put two beers down in front of Uriah and Sam, slamming them on the table a little harder than was necessary. Doc paid him and he went off again. Doc looked at Uriah Van Hawley again. ''I take it you came here to Tamarack Springs because so many outlaws drift in and out of here, and that way you can get their stories, is that it?''

''Precisely,'' said Uriah. ''Teaching school back in Missouri left me bored and restless. I'd prospected in these parts when I was young, and always wanted to return. One day I simply dropped everything and did just that.''

Doc was thoughtful. ''Then if somebody wanted information on these various, uh, temporary residents of the Springs, you'd be the man to come to, is that right?''

Sam Ruby looked at him sharply. ''You're looking for information like that?''

''Just interested,'' said Doc, passing it off. ''Nothing special. Enjoy your beers, gents. I'd better rejoin my partner before he gets into trouble. Which,'' he added with a grin, ''he has a way of doing.''

Raider was still at their table behind the potted plant, staring around the big room rather morosely. Doc knew that look of his: With not much to do, Raider was ready for a prolonged bout with either whiskey or women, or maybe both. Doc sat and told Raider about the two chess players; Raider shrugged as though to say he figured Doc was wasting his time talking to them. In rebuttal, Doc said, ''You never know who's gonna be useful. You blow into a strange place, it's always wise to talk to as many people as possible. That's how you learn what's going on.''

"Well, you go ahead and gab all you want, Doc," said Raider. "I might just mosey on down to the firehouse and see if maybe Claudette can't get away a spell."

Doc grinned. "There's not many gals you go back to for seconds. Don't tell me you're getting sweet on her."

"I don't get sweet on *nobody*," growled Raider.

As they talked, they were at first only vaguely aware that a man had entered the saloon hastily, slapping trail dust from his trousers with his hat, and then bustling up to the bar to ask a hurried question of the sad-eyed bartender. A moment after that, he turned and strode across the room to the table where Doc and Raider sat.

Doc and Raider looked up at him. His blond hair would have been almost white had it been clean, but it was greasy with sweat, and, unbarbered for maybe a month of Sundays, it hung down almost to his shoulders. His fair skin was reddened and roughened, rather than tanned, by the sun, and his eyes were pale, with a surly, challenging look. "You two the new vets?" he asked.

"I'm Doc Weatherbee, yes. This is my assistant, Raider."

"Well, get your asses out to the XL, quick. Miz Larkin needs you out there."

Raider stared back at the man evenly. "You ever hear of the word 'please,' mister? Or didn't you ever have no ma to teach it to you?"

The pale eyes became colder as the man held them on Raider. "You pokin' fun at me?"

"If that's what you figure," Raider said calmly. "You want to make somethin' out of it, you go right ahead. I was just thinkin' things are too damn quiet around here, anyway."

The man put his hands on his hips—which, of course, brought his right hand nearer his gun, holstered somewhat low on his thigh. "You know who you're talkin' to?"

"Don't know and don't give a jackrabbit turd," said Raider.

"You must be *real* new around here," the man said. "I'm Clay Dillard, the XL foreman."

"Don't care if you're the Queen of Juh-pip'," said Raider.

Doc frowned. "Now, hold on, both of you. Looks to me like there's some unnecessary misunderstanding here. The fact is, Mr. Dillard, we haven't heard of you, and if you'll simmer down an minute and think about it, you'll see there's no reason why we should have. As for my partner, Raider, he's not looking to tangle horns with a stranger just for the hell of it, but he doesn't like folks walking up to him and issuing commands out of a clear blue sky. I don't expect you'd like that either. Now. Shall we start all over again, and do it right this time?"

Dillard scowled for a moment, absorbing what Doc had said. "Well," he said finally, "maybe I better spell it out, seein' as you two don't know who's who in these parts. I work for Rina Larkin—she owns the XL, the biggest spread around here. When she asks a favor, folks usually oblige. She pays for what she gets, and she pays good. She heard you two blew into town, and she needs your services. Right quick."

"What seems to be the trouble?"

"Her prize dairy cow. She had it shipped out here all the way from Kansas City, and it cost more'n a whole damn herd of regular whitefaces. She was figurin' on breedin up from it, but if the damn critter ups and dies now, all that expense goes for nothin'."

"I see," said Doc. "What are the symptoms?"

"Won't eat, don't want to stand. Bellowin' like somethin' hurts inside. Been three days like that. You'll see when you get there. Miz Larkin said bring you two back right away."

"Did *she* say please?" asked Doc.

"Huh?" said Dillard.

"If she didn't, you're going back alone."

Again it took a moment to sink in. Then Dillard said,

"Well, I reckon she *sort* of said it. I reckon she meant it, anyway."

"In that case," said Raider, rising from his chair, "I reckon we can ride out with you and take a look."

As Clay Dillard, slouched on a dappled mare, led the way, Doc and Raider turned the wagon from the main road and through a gateway with the XL brand on its high crossbeam. From here, a winding trail led through rolling hills to a broad hollow where the ranch buildings lay. The main house was low and rambling, much of it built of mortared rock; Dillard brought them past this and directly to the barn.

Inside, the prize dairy cow was on its side, its flanks heaving with what appeared to be labored breathing. Raider, who had been raised on a farm in Arkansas, saw at once that it was a magnificent cow, though he had no particular fondness for cattle in any form—unless maybe a good sizzling steak, broiled just right on an open fire.

"That's her," said Dillard, nodding. "Name's Duchess. Which she's just about as expensive as."

Doc leaned over the creature and went through the motions of inspecting it closely, starting with its mouth and eyes, then patting and poking it gently here and there all the way down to its immense, swelling udder. Presently he rose and showed the foreman a grave expression.

"She's got a rare disease," he said. "Bucolitis. Not many vets who could treat it, but fortunately I'm one who can. You go tell that lady boss of yours it's gonna take some time."

Dillard looked puzzled, ran his hand through his scraggly blond hair, then finally frowned, turned, and left the barn.

Raider looked at Doc. "What the hell's bucolitis? Never heard of it before."

"That's because there's no such thing," said Doc blithely.

"What?" Raider stared.

"Made it up on the spot," said Doc. "Bucolitis. Sounds

scary, doesn't it? I must remember it—might want to use it again sometime.''

"Doc, have you plumb lost your mind?"

"Not at all," said Doc. "And it so happens I'm practicing medicine like I learned it when I was a vet's assistant. A certain part of it, anyway."

"You get harder and harder to figure out," said Raider, narrowing his eyes on his partner.

"There were lots of times," Doc said patiently, "when this sawbones I worked for couldn't figure out what was wrong with some critter. That's partly because critters can't talk and tell you where they hurt, and partly because they're always getting things wrong with them that don't seem to be in any book. When this happened, the old fellow would look very wise, tell the owner he had a real sick animal, and then maybe give it a pill that couldn't hurt it—but of course couldn't help it any, either. If the critter died, he'd say, 'See? Told you it was serious.' If the critter recovered—and often enough, it would, just naturally—he'd take credit for the cure.''

"I see." Raider was thoughtful. "Well, you're takin' a helluva chance, Doc. If this damn cow kicks off—which it looks to me like it's gonna do—this Larkin woman ain't gonna be too happy about it. And it ain't gonna do much for our reputation here. I've got the feelin', Doc, we're doin' everything wrong this time. Maybe we better figure out some way to pull in our horns and start all over again.''

Doc shook his head. "This is no time to give up. We haven't even gotten started yet. There's something mighty strange going on—something connected with those fires somebody set—and the only way we're going to find out what it is is by asking questions. Rina Larkin seems to be in the thick of it, and she's one person we've got to talk to. In fact, it was a stroke of luck she called us in to look at this cow. Gives us a good excuse to get next to her.''

"Well, I don't know," said Raider, with a doubtful frown.

"Rade," said Doc, "stop worrying and follow my lead. Right now, I'll stay with Duchess a spell, like I was curing her of what ails her. You go on up to the house and sweet-talk this Larkin woman, so we'll be sure to have her on our side. Get romantic with her, if you have to. These baggy old widows usually respond to a little of that."

"What the hell do you think I am? Some stud that gets let out for breedin'?"

Doc grinned. "Close to it. Anyway, you do like I say and we might just start learning some more about whatever it is we're trying to find out."

Raider's frown deepened. "Well," he said reluctantly, "I'll talk to the old gal—but if you think I'm gonna romance her, you got another think comin'. I'll tumble in the hay with anything that's halfway pretty, especially when I've got a powerful hard-on, but when it comes to old widows and such, I draw the line."

"You ought to take Ben Franklin's advice," said Doc.

"Ben Franklin again? What's he got to do with it?"

"He wrote a letter to a young man giving eight reasons why he should choose an older woman for a mistress. The general idea was she'd have more experience and give him a better time all around."

Raider shook his head sadly. "Ben Franklin must have been as loco as you are, Doc. See you later."

The main house of the XL was a well-built structure with the grounds in its immediate vicinity nicely kept; there was a flower garden along the base of the porch and a stand of poplars to mark off a kind of courtyard area where the road from the distant gateway ended.

Clay Dillard sat on the steps to the porch, cleaning his sixgun. Its belt and holster lay beside him, and he was running a rag soaked with whale oil through the chambers of its removed cylinder.

He looked up as Raider approached. His expression seemed annoyed, but Raider expected it always did; the entire world, Dillard seemed to feel, was out there to keep him from doing exactly what he wanted to do at any given time. He'd evidently had time to comb out his stringy blond hair and change to a freshly laundered shirt, and with this much grooming he looked much more presentable. Raider had the idea he'd slicked himself up this much for the benefit of his widowed employer.

"Miz Larkin here?" asked Raider.

"Yup." Dillard nodded. "But she's busy. How's that cow comin' along?"

"That's what I wanna talk to her about."

"You talk to me about it," said Dillard. "I'm the one runs the ranch."

"Well," Raider answered mildly, "she's the one owns the cow. So it's gotta be her I talk to."

"You don't hear so good, do you, Raider?" Dillard laid down his gun and rose. There was something lithe and languid in his movements that signaled a readiness to enforce any request or command he happened to put out, and maybe that made him a good foreman, but he seemed to forget that Raider wasn't one of his hands. "If everybody who wanted to get next to Rina could, she'd be all day socializin' instead of gettin' work done. So just speak your piece, whatever it is."

Raider smiled a little. "Tell you what, Dillard. If Rina says talk to you, that's what I'll do. But first I gotta hear Rina herself say it."

He stepped forward to mount the steps. Dillard blocked his way. "You're new in these parts, Raider. So I'll overlook this uppity way of yours. Let's get it straight. Your business is with that sick cow and me and nobody else. Keep it that way and you'll save yourself some trouble."

"Dillard," said Raider calmly, "I'm steppin' up to that front door, and I'm gonna knock on it nice and polite and ask for Rina Larkin. Can't imagine why anyone would want to stop me from doin' a little thing like that, but if anybody tried I reckon he's the one who'd find himself some trouble.''

As Raider had known he would—as both men had known for several moments now—Dillard lashed out with a swift, hooking punch. Raider dodged it easily, but not the blow with Dillard's other hand that followed it and caught Raider in the solar plexus, making him gasp and bend forward. When he did that a third punch came out of the air and caught him on the side of the jaw.

Raider wasn't often caught by surprise, and he cussed himself now for underestimating Clay Dillard. Somewhere along the line the man had learned to handle his fists pretty fancy. Little zigzag flashes appeared for an instant before Raider's eyes when his jaw was struck, but his own fists were already in motion, and he brought a hard uppercut to the point of Dillard's chin, catching it square, snapping the foreman's head back and making him stumble away. Raider came forward, pressing his advantage, as Dillard recovered quickly and started throwing punches again.

Both men stood toe to toe, swinging. Each man ducked or dodged some of the punches, but failed to avoid just as many. Raider saw a cut open on Dillard's cheekbone. He suddenly tasted salt and knew his own lip had been cut.

And then, partly by luck, and partly because he'd waited for exactly the right opening, Raider got in a short, hard right that traveled the optimum distance and had just the right amount of leverage behind it. It also caught Dillard's jaw in what must have been just the right place. The foreman's eyes glassed over and his knees buckled. Raider readied another punch to make him fall.

''That's enough, you two!'' came a woman's voice from the porch.

Raider looked up and saw Xavierina Larkin. He wasn't sure how he knew her for the owner of the XL, because she wasn't at all what he had expected. She was tall, fulsome of build, her bosom and hips in solid curves. She wore a mannish checked shirt and a long gray riding skirt with a buttoned slit in front. Her tiny waist was pinched in by a concha belt of heavy silver and turquoise.

Raider stared at her for a second, then said, "Howdy, ma'am."

"All right," said Rina, her dark eyes snapping back and forth between the two men, "just what in hell is going on here?"

"He was tryin' to bust in," said Dillard.

"Damn right," said Raider. "It's about that cow of yours. I figure you're the one to hear, not this glorified cowpoke of yours."

At that, Dillard started forward toward Raider again, until Rina said sharply, "Hold it, Clay!" She looked at Raider again. "You're the new veterinarian?"

"Doc Weatherbee is. He's with the cow now. I'm his partner. Name's Raider."

"All right, Mr. Raider. I'll have you know Mr. Dillard is following my orders, which are to keep people from bothering me with details about the ranch. At the same time I think both of you are acting like a couple of silly kids to let it get out of hand like this. But we'll let that go for the time being. Clay, you go on about your business, and Mr. Raider, you step into the house. Afterward, I don't want you tangling again. That's an order that goes for the two of you."

Moments later Raider was in a large, well-furnished room dominated by a fireplace that took up the greater part of one wall. Rina showed him to a wide lounge seat upholstered in brocaded silk. She stood there, looking down at him after he was seated, and he could see her dark eyes flickering back and forth as she studied him in detail. He couldn't pin down her age—anything from mid-thirties to mid-forties—but whatever it was, it hadn't yet brought the first noticeable wrinkle to her skin, which had the color and texture of dark, polished ivory. Raider had the impression that he was looking at more pure woman than was usually packed into one person.

"You've got a cut lip there, Mr. Raider," she said. "Stay right where you are; I'll fix it up for you."

"Don't bother. It ain't all that much."

She turned to rummage for a moment in the drawer of a desklike table, from which she retrived a ball of cotton. When she came back toward Raider again she also had a bottle of whiskey in her hand. "You're right," she said, "it's not very serious. Which is unusual for anyone who's just tangled with Clay Dillard. I've seen him handle some pretty big men. And he's as good with a gun as he is with his fists. You're lucky I stopped that little dogfight of yours."

Raider shrugged. "Maybe he's the lucky one."

Rina, who was daubing Raider's cut with the whiskey-soaked cotton now, showed a slight smile. "You seem pretty confident of yourself, Mr. Raider. I heard how you and your partner saved the fire engine for us. I hope you're both as good veterinarians as you seem to be brawlers."

"Well, it's Doc who's the veterinarian," Raider said, "and I reckon he knows his stuff as well as anybody. What he wants me to tell you is that this prize cow of yours has a real rare disease. Some long name I forget for the moment. But Doc says he's one of the few men in the country who knows what to do about it."

"Is Duchess going to recover?"

"That's what he's not too sure of. He's workin' on her now and it looks like it might take some time. He asked me to let you know about it so you won't be too surprised if Duchess don't come out of it."

"I see." Attending to the cut on Raider's lip, Rina had been bent over him and near enough to him for him to feel her body warmth. He'd also been able to look down the front of her shirt, open by several buttons at the neck, and see the line of separation between her great swelling breasts.

It came to him that Rina was more than a full measure of what he liked, all in one package.

She straightened herself now, returning the cork to the whiskey bottle. He noticed that she was still inspecting him with interest, even though she had already had her first good survey. "Kind of a shame to waste whiskey that good on a cut," drawled Raider.

Rina smiled. "It is good whiskey, Mr. Raider—"

"Hardly anybody calls me mister. And if I ever had a first name, I forgot it. Just make it 'Raider,' okay?"

"All right, Raider. The whiskey's from Tennessee. My late husband used to have it shipped here by the case. The same as he did back in Texas, before we came here. Nothing but the best for Ben Larkin, while he was alive, and I've tried to continue that way. Let me pour you a little of this sourmash."

"Why, thank you, ma'am."

"Make it Rina."

He smiled as she fetched a glass and poured. "I heard you run the XL all by yourself—and also that you do a good job of it."

"Things have gone well enough. Mostly it's plain hard work. But that's all right. The busier I keep, the less time I have to get lonely."

"A woman with your looks shouldn't be lonely. I'd think all sorts of hombres would be pantin' after you."

She laughed a little. "Me, or this spread of mine. It's always hard to tell which. Anyway, if I ever hitch up again it's got to be with somebody who's man enough to measure up to Ben."

"Does that foreman of yours think he fits the bill?"

"Never mind Clay Dillard. He does his job and does it well. That's enough. And I hope"—she steadied her look upon him—"I hope *you're* not getting ideas like the rest of them."

"None I didn't already have," said Raider, grinning, sipping his whiskey.

She cocked her head. "Frankly, Raider, I'm not sure just how to peg you. Maybe, as time goes on, we'll get better acquainted. I understand you and your partner figure on settling down here. You could do worse. Tamarack Springs is going to grow when they build that railroad spur up from Yancy. Someday there'll be a city here big as Denver, or maybe even Chicago. Some folks in town still can't see it, but they'll be coming around eventually. Men like Winfield Brent are just going to be left behind."

"I heard you and him didn't hit it off too well."

Rina shrugged. "He wants the Springs to continue as a haven for outlaws, which, of course, is where his profit lies. But if this town's going to grow it'll have to be respectable and attract the right kind of people. Those who settle down and open businesses and, above all, pay taxes, so we can have everything a proper town needs. I have a stake in the town because I've had what I hope is the foresight to acquire a few businesses and some property here and there. But even more than that, I want to see it grow. The way Ben did when he was alive."

Trying to sound casual, Raider said, "Just how much has Winfield Brent been getting in your way?"

"What do you mean?" She looked at him a little suspiciously.

"Well, Doc and I just blew in, of course, but we've heard rumors. Like, maybe some of the recent fires you had weren't all by accident. If they put people out of business they could maybe keep the town from growing. Which is what Brent wants—right?"

She frowned. "Raider, I don't think we ought to be talking about things like this. Not yet, anyway. Let's wait till I know a little bit more about you and, of course, vice versa."

Raider rose suddenly. He brought his hands forward and put them on her swelling hips, just below her tight waist. He eased her toward himself, pressed his outthrust pelvis to hers, and then touched his lips to her parted lips. She remained stock still and kept her eyes open but, he noticed, did not freeze entirely. Her lips moved just a little under his, as though, separately and alone, they were extending an invitation. When she did not respond fully, however, Raider stepped back quietly. "If we're gonna get better acquainted," he said, "now's as good a time as any to start."

Her faint smile showed that at least she was not angry. "Some things shouldn't be rushed, Raider. And don't take that as any kind of a promise. I'll be honest with you. I'm not a blushing virgin, but I'm not a silly, middle-aged woman desperate for affection, either. If you turn out to be the man I think you are—as time goes on—well, we'll take another look at it. Until then, just keep things the way they are, all right?"

Raider shrugged. "Okay, I can wait. I always can, when there's somethin' worth waitin' for."

There was a knock on the door. Rina went to answer it while Raider stood there, finishing his whiskey, and a moment later she returned with Doc in tow.

Doc looked around the room, and then at Raider. "Hope I'm not interrupting anything," he said dryly.

"You ain't," growled Raider. "And it wouldn't be your business if you were."

CHAPTER NINE

Doc now had his own tumbler of Tennessee whiskey in his hand and was sipping it with pleasure. The three of them were arranged almost formally in the room, Doc and Raider on a davenport and Xavierina Larkin seated almost primly in an armchair across from them.

"I'm delighted to hear that Duchess is on her feet again," said Rina. "How did you do it?"

"If you'll forgive me, ma'am," said Doc smoothly, "the treatment must remain a secret. It's still experimental, and I can't let it be known until I've tested it more thoroughly."

Raider looked at his partner sharply. A certain well-oiled tone came into Doc's voice whenever he was bullshitting, and it was there now. It was Raider's guess that the animal had recovered naturally, as Doc had said it might—in fact, given Doc's somewhat less than perfect knowledge of veterinary medicine, that was the only possible explanation.

Rina had poured herself a glass of wine; she regarded both men quietly across the rim of it. "Gentlemen," she said, "now that you're here, and now that Duchess seems to be all right, you might as well know that I wasn't sure about you at first. Strangers in Tamarack Springs are apt to be anything from mountebanks to downright killers. But with Duchess apparently ready to expire, I had to take a chance. Now I'm beginning to think that perhaps you might be able to do more for the community than taking care of a few sick animals."

"Like what, ma'am?" Doc asked cautiously.

"I've heard you two can take care of yourselves. I've even witnessed Raider in action, more or less. He's as bad as Clay Dillard when it comes to holding his temper, and the both of them ought to be spanked." Her slight smile softened what she was saying. "At any rate, I believe we can use men of your particular talents on our side. Winfield Brent has all those gunfighters he can call on, so it's time we had our own little force. Just in case."

Doc studied the whiskey in his glass. "You're expecting trouble?"

"There's already been trouble. The fires—which you evidently know about. A while ago Raider mentioned what must be obvious—that it would be in Brent's interest to start those fires, though we haven't any proof that he did. And then we have the two attacks on the fire engine. All of it adds up to too much for just plain coincidence. And it gives us good reason to think there might be a showdown one of these days. That's when we'll be needing men like you."

"Maybe so." Raider frowned. "But Doc and I hadn't really figured on steppin' into a fight and takin' sides."

"If you're going to stay, you'll have to take one side or the other," Rina said. "It's boiled down to that now. The only other choice is to turn tail and go back where you came from. And somehow I don't think you're that kind."

"Maybe not," said Raider. "But this is still somethin' we've got to think about."

Rina rose and set her wineglass down on the sideboard. "I think it's time you both met some of the folks in our Civic Improvement Group. I'm giving a dinner party for them Saturday evening at seven. May I count on your company?"

"Our pleasure, ma'am," said Doc, nodding as though bowing. He stood and said to Raider, "Coming along, or are you gonna sit there all day?"

Rina showed them to the door and stood there, smiling as they stalked to the wagon, mounted it, and headed down the long, winding driveway to the main road. Just before they got out of sight, Raider switched around to look back and saw Rina waving good-bye. Doc slapped the reins on Judith's back, and the mule twitched her ears and picked up the pace a little.

The afternoon sun was mellow in a clear blue sky. The only clouds in sight were cottonball puffs over distant peaks along the horizon. Judith plodded along, no faster than she had to, which Doc considered a mark of her intelligence. A dumb mule, he believed, was still smarter than a smart horse, though he could never convince Raider of this.

He glanced at Raider now with a somewhat sly grin on his lips. "How was she, Rade? Pretty good, like Ben Franklin said?"

"None o' your damn business, Doc," growled Raider.

Doc laughed. "Well, I won't press the matter. What we'd better be thinking about now is what to do next. If Brent's really behind those fires, the insurance company would be mighty happy to see him stopped and put away in the hoosegow for a while. Trouble is, we don't really know enough about Brent or any of his crowd to give us an idea of how to handle him."

"Maybe we could make him think we're hidin' out from the law too," said Raider. "Pretend like we're joinin' up with him. We've played it that way before."

Doc shook his head quickly. "It's likely that wouldn't work this time. Too many professional criminals from all parts of the country hanging around Brent. They know who's been robbing banks and gunning folks down and that kind of thing. If we claim we were in on some job somewhere, there's a good chance one of them would know we weren't. In fact, I've been a little worried one of them might up and recognize us as Pinkerton operatives. We've got ourselves a reputation, you know, same as they have.''

''Maybe so,'' said Raider, nodding. ''Goddamn, I thought this job was gonna be real simple. What the hell did we get ourselves into this time, anyway?''

Doc leaned back for a moment as he continued to turn the situation over in his mind. ''Remember those two old farts who were playing chess? One of them—Uriah Van Hawley—is a kind of professor, as I understand it, and he's been putting together this history of western outlaws. He came here to do it because there's so many around he can talk to. He'd be the one to tell us just who's here, and what they've been up to.''

''What good would that do us?''

''I'm not sure,'' said Doc, still wrestling with his thought and showing it in his frown. ''It's maybe a shot in the dark, but it's occurred to me if there's a firebug among these hombres, and he's doing Brent's dirty work, well, he'd be the one to watch.''

''You're reachin' hard, Doc,'' Raider said doubtfully.

''Better than not reaching at all,'' Doc said, shrugging. ''Van Hawley's got a cabin out in the hills somewhere. What do you say we ride out and visit him in the morning?''

''Guess it wouldn't do harm,'' said Raider. ''Though I don't see as it'll do much good, either.''

They rode on silently for a while. Raider dozed. Doc glanced at him, resenting both his ability to catch a few winks of sleep anytime, anywhere, and the fact that Doc had to stay awake to do the driving. Judith, who sensed Doc's fondness for her, just wouldn't answer to Raider the way she would to Doc, and could get real stubborn about it.

The road took a sharp bend through a stand of loosely scattered cottonwoods. They were throwing dappled shade down on the dusty, ochre soil. Doc was in the middle of a yawn when suddenly the wagon was surrounded by riders who seemed to have appeared out of thin air.

Instantly alert, both Doc and Raider, in reflex action, reached for their holstered weapons.

"Wouldn't do that if I was you, boys," said a drawling voice.

Doc and Raider saw at once that several rifles and revolvers, in the hands of men who probably knew how to use them, were pointed their way, which made what the man had said sound advice. They recognized him immediately, though not by name. He was thin, rangy, and slouched down in his saddle as though he meant to stay in it for a day or two; he was the same man who had twice led an attack on the fire engine—the man, in fact, whose gun Raider had shot from his hand during the second attempt. And his five companions were those who had been with him before. As before, all had covered their faces with bandanas tied just below their eyes.

"First thing," said the rangy man, "you take off your gunbelts real slow and careful. Then you drop 'em over the side. And after that your hands go way up, like you was airin' 'em out to dry."

When they had reluctantly complied with that order, Doc said, "You mind telling us what this is all about?"

The rangy man's voice sounded as though he were grinning under his bandana. "Don't mind at all. Me and my friends here, we're workin' part-time as messenger boys. That's what we're doin'. Bringin' you two a little message."

"From who?"

"That's up to you to guess. Now step on down from the wagon."

As Doc and Raider descended from their perch they inspected the six riders even more closely, trying to place them as persons they might have seen in the Grand Palace or elsewhere around the town. They were a mixed group who might have sallied out of any cow camp; none seemed familiar. The smallest among them—Doc would bet he was called Shorty—had already dismounted and scooped up their gunbelts from the dust. He stepped toward the rangy man and held them out.

"Here you are, Gouch."

"Hang on to 'em, you damn fool!" said the rangy man.

Doc brought his head up. "Gouch," he said. "Now that's an interesting nickname. From the gouch hook a cook uses to lift pot lids, I imagine. You must have been a trail cook before. You should've stuck to it. It's healthier than playing with guns and dynamite."

The man's eyes—they were almost yellow, like a wolf's—glared at Doc across the top of his bandana. "What I heard about you was right, Weatherbee. You got a real busy mouth. It ain't gonna help you much this time, though."

Raider also glanced at Doc with a slight frown. He knew what Doc was up to—putting out a cloud of talk, the way he sometimes did, could puzzle an opponent and put him off balance so that a quick play could be made, but this just didn't seem a good time for that particular tactic. Truth was, Gouch and his companions had the drop on them good and proper, and, as far as Raider could see, there wasn't a damn thing they could do about it.

Gouch now unforked himself from the saddle, and, as though this had been a signal, the others dismounted too. He turned first to Shorty, who was still standing there with a stupid air, holding Doc's and Raider's weapons, and apparently still wondering what to do with them.

"Shorty," Gouch said—Doc had been right about the small man's inevitable handle—"keep an eye on these two while we unhitch that mule. If either one of 'em makes even a tiny move, you let 'em have some lead. Right in the balls would be a real good place."

Shorty continued to seem faintly bewildered as he hooked the gunbelts over one arm, drew his own weapon with the other, and pointed it at Doc and Raider.

As a puzzled Doc and Raider watched, Gouch and the

others stepped toward the wagon and busied themselves unfastening the harness that held Judith to the forks. Not liking these strangers handling her, Judith snorted and sidestepped; one of the men cursed her and grabbed her bridle, pinching down hard on the curb bit.

Gouch swung away from these operations and returned to where Doc and Raider were standing. "There's a drop down the road a piece," he said in a tone of voice he might have used for pleasant conversation. "Maybe you noticed. Bunch o' rocks there like you might find rattle-snakes in. That's where the wagon's goin'. Over the side and into them rocks. I expect it's gonna bust it up some."

"I expect it might," Raider said calmly. "But tell me this. What the hell good does that do you?"

"It's the message we got for you," said Gouch. "If you can't read it so good, I'll spell it out for you. There's a certain gentleman you two was supposed to report to. Seems like you didn't get around to it. Now, this here gentleman, he gets upset when folks don't keep their appointments. What he wants you to understand is that when somebody crosses him, he don't just let it drop."

"Winfield Brent, huh? So he's the one who sent you coyotes out to blow up that fire engine. Figured as much."

"Well, you just keep on figurin', Raider," said Gouch. "And maybe after a while you'll figure how it's best to play by the rules here in Tamarack Springs."

Two of the other men were now looping lariat lengths of three-eighths whale line to the fork of the wagon so that several riders would be able to drag it at high speed and let it go, careening and tumbling, when they came to the drop alongside the road. A second pair were trying to lead Judith, stiff-legged and balking, off to one side. Gouch turned away again, evidently to lend assistance.

Doc threw a quick glance at Raider, who, at that moment, had also turned his eyes toward Doc. They'd been together long enough to understand each other's quick glances. This one said, as clearly as though Doc had spoken the words, "Get ready for a play!"

Almost instantly, Raider saw what the play would be. Two men busy at the wagon, Gouch heading toward them, and two others trying to drag Judith away from it—which made five of them not looking at Doc and Raider for the moment. The sixth man was Shorty, who still had his hogleg pointed at them. And Shorty looked to be a man with the reflexes of a tortoise, or maybe even a mite slower than that.

"Judith!" Doc called out sharply. "You come here!"

As Raider well knew, Doc hadn't really trained Judith to come trotting when he called, like a dog might do. But he'd tried to do it so many times that she always responded to his voice—if only to lurch away stubbornly in the opposite direction. That was what she did now, rearing back from the men who were pulling at her, and, when she found she couldn't bring her head up, kicking out with her hind legs.

It was the momentary distraction Raider and Doc needed. Even Shorty had turned his head to look at all the commotion Judith was raising behind him. Raider and Doc threw themselves forward, crashed into Shorty, knocked him flying into the dust, and grabbed their gunbelts as they dropped from his arm. It all happened so fast that Gouch and his men scarcely had time to blink at it. Suddenly, and to their surprise, Doc and Raider were both in a crouch, with Raider's .44 and Doc's Diamondback pointed at them.

One man at the fork of the wagon reached for his gun. Raider's Remington, which he always felt hefted better in his hand than the more popular Colt .45, spoke instantly, and the man spun around hard, grabbing at his upper arm.

"Who's next?" Raider called out. "One little move— that's all I got to see!"

They made stone statues of themselves, wherever they stood.

"That's better," Raider said. "Okay, Doc. You can collect iron now."

Moments later Doc had all their weapons in a pile at his and Raider's feet. He pointed his Diamondback again and said, "Bunch up, boys. Where we can see you all at once."

They shuffled together into a closer group, the man Raider had shot still holding his arm and looking with pained surprise at the blood seeping up between his fingers. Gouch, in the middle of the group, glared at Doc and Raider venomously. Shorty looked blank, as though he still hadn't figured out exactly what had happened.

"Pull them bandanas down," said Raider. "I want a good look at all you varmints."

They obeyed. Gouch's face turned out to be hollow-cheeked and weak-chinned. Shorty had a bushy mustache under his stubby nose. The others were of mixed descriptions, one bearded, one with heavy jowls, another swarthy and Spanish-looking, still another with peach fuzz on his upper lip and the mean face of a boy trying to prove he was just as tough and nasty as any full-grown man could be. The man Raider had shot in the arm seemed older than the rest, his unshaven stubble showing flecks of silver here and there.

His eyes still on all of them, Raider said to Doc, "Anybody here you seen before?"

"Don't believe so," said Doc. "Though I expect we could find most of them on a reward poster someplace."

"All right, you sorry bunch o' polecats," said Raider, "I'm gonna make a little speech, which is somethin' I don't usually do, but I figure this time it's called for. If there's one thing Doc and I admire, it's to be left the hell alone. I got half a mind to gut-shoot every one of you here and now, just to be sure you won't be botherin' us again. I never shot an unarmed man yet, but there's always a first time, so don't get your hopes too high. I ain't made up my mind yet, but if I do let you skedaddle out of here alive, you'd better make up *your* minds to one real important thing. Next time you see Doc and me comin' down the street, get out of our way. And don't figure on tryin' to dry-gulch us, either—we got eyes in the back of our heads.''

"Look, Raider," said Gouch, frowning, "we got nothin' personal against you two. We were just followin' orders. Same as you'll be doin' if you stick around these parts. There ain't no way out of it—not if a man wants to stay here and be safe.''

"That may be so for your kind," Raider said. "But it don't apply to Doc and me. Looks like you and Brent and everybody else figure we're on the owl hoot too. You go back and tell Brent we don't need his protection, and if he keeps peckerin' on us, *he's* the one who'll need to be protected.''

Gouch stared back, unbelieving. "I'll tell him that, Raider, but I don't expect he's gonna swaller it down. Anybody who can handle a gun like you two ain't no ordinary citizen. Leastwise not in my experience.''

"In that case, you ain't had enough experience yet. But I'm not gonna argue with you all day. Get on your nags, all of you, and ride out of here without even lookin' back. And figure yourselves lucky you're gettin' out alive. And that makes enough talk for today. Go on—git!''

They moved with surly expressions and slowly at first, until both Doc and Raider gestured with their guns to hurry them along. Moments later they had mounted, and, with one or two of them daring to glare back in anger, they broke into a gallop, headed for town. Doc and Raider watched until they disappeared.

"I don't like it," said Doc, frowning. "We're gonna have to step mighty careful from now on.''

"Maybe," said Raider, nodding. "But at least we know a little better what Winfield Brent's up to. He was the one who tried to keep that fire engine from gettin' here—just like we thought.''

Doc's face was slightly contorted, the way it always was when he was trying to unravel an intricate puzzle. "There's still something that bothers me about the whole queersome setup," he said. "I can understand that Brent wants to keep on taking care of all the outlaws that drift this way—they probably pay him well for it. But is it all that big, business-wise? Is he making that much of a fortune out of it? With that hotel and saloon he owns, he might have just as much to gain as everybody else if the town grows and turns into a big cattle-shipping center. And those fires Rina and Ormsby figure he had somebody start for him. Think about it, Rade. They might be a pain in the ass for everybody, but are they *really* going to stop the town from growing? I'd say they'd be likely to do just the opposite—which is make Rina and her crowd even more stubborn and determined to build up Tamarack Springs in spite of all hell."

"Doc," said Raider, "you got a way of makin' things more complexified than they are."

"I don't know about that," said Doc. "The real explanation may turn out to be quite simple. So simple it's right under our noses and we can't see it. And I don't think we'll see it till we know a lot more about Brent and all the temporary residents he's got holed up here."

"Well," Raider drawled, "you go ahead and bust your brains over it, if you want. But meantime gimme a hand hitchin' up the wagon so we can get back to town. We'll try again tomorrow."

CHAPTER TEN

The foothills were heavily wooded, and now, in the early morning, there were traces of blue mist in the sharp little valleys and draws that lay among them. With this much cover all around them, Doc and Raider rode carefully, their eyes constantly sweeping their surroundings, alert for any sign of movement that might seem out of place.

Once, several deer broke for a wooded patch and bounded up the side of a long slope—flushed by a cougar, for a guess, though they never saw the predator itself. Ahead at the crest of a hill, an eagle soared off, annoyed, as a flock of crows—western crows, almost as big as buzzards—dipped and swooped all around it, screaming in anger but doing little damage. These were sudden interruptions, and they made Doc and Raider pause and stiffen themselves in their saddles, but they were also natural movements that might be expected at this time, when most wild creatures were hunting and feeding.

"Maybe we shouldn't have rode out here," said Raider, frowning.

"Maybe," said Doc. "But it's better than doing nothing—and waiting for Brent to make another play."

They had risen at dawn, meaning to slip out of the boardinghouse before breakfast time, but Ma Ormsby had heard them and, coming downstairs in an old bathrobe, had insisted on making toast and coffee for them. The night before, they'd sat in the parlor and listened to Ab Ormsby's rambling tales of fighting fires in Chicago. Several times Raider had stirred restlessly, and Doc had thought he'd been ready to suggest that they wander down to the Grand Palace for a drink or two, but Doc had looked at him sharply to remind him what they'd already agreed upon—that they wouldn't give Brent the satisfaction of seeming to heed the warning he'd sent them in the attempt to wreck their wagon.

As for Doc, he'd had a good night's sleep for a change. Heather had been at choir practice most of the evening, getting home late, and when she didn't sneak into Doc's room in the dark of morning, Doc figured she was either genuinely tired or had already satisfied herself with one of her regular boyfriends.

"There's one thing we can be sure of," said Raider, still scanning the slopes as their horses moved along at a brisk walk. "Brent ain't finished tryin' to scare us off."

Doc nodded. "Maybe even more than that. His reputation's at stake now. I've got an idea he might like to see us buried. Which is why we rode out early—so he wouldn't know we'd be in a position to get ourselves dry-gulched again."

"Just the same," Raider said thoughtfully, "don't count on his not knowin'. I wouldn't be surprised if he had a man watchin' the boardinghouse all night. I didn't see no sign of it, but I still wouldn't be surprised."

"Hold on, Rade," said Doc, peering ahead. "That must be Van Hawley's place up there. This is about where Ab said it would be."

Raider squinted in the same direction. A thin column of blue smoke rose from the trees perhaps a hundred yards up a steep hillside. Raider looked at it for a moment, nodded, and then both men swung their horses toward it, heeling their flanks gently.

With the horses straining and snorting softly a few

times, they mounted the steep incline, riding through the tall, straight pines that held the dark loam in place against erosion. A tumbling creek off to one side told them why Uriah Van Hawley had chosen to build his cabin in this particular spot.

Moments later the cabin, sitting in a natural clearing, was in sight. It was made of notched pine logs caulked with clay; a wide stone chimney, from which the smoke was rising, formed most of the wall at one end. A short distance from it stood a small, boothlike structure with a half-moon cut into its flimsy door, to show that Uriah had included all the comforts of home in his sanctuary.

The door to the cabin was open. Doc and Raider dismounted, and Doc called out, "Anybody home?"

A small stone came hurtling through the air from somewhere behind them and dropped on the ground near their feet. Startled, both men whirled, reaching for their guns. They stopped reaching when they saw the two barrels of a shotgun gaping at them from a distance of only several yards.

A girl held the shotgun. It was clear enough that she'd concealed herself in the trees as they had approached, then stepped out from behind them so that she'd have the advantage. And the way she held the shotgun—steady as could be—suggested that she meant to use that advantage for all it was worth if that turned out to be necessary.

"Howdy, miss," said Raider, his hand still hooked in midair, halfway to his holster.

Her reaction was curious, and it took a moment for Raider and Doc to understand what she meant by it. With her right hand still on the triggers, she took her left hand from the barrels of the gun, waggled it in the air for a moment, then pointed skyward with her finger.

"Huh?" said Raider, staring.

"I believe she wants us to reach," said Doc mildly.

Hearing that, the girl nodded and pointed upward again.

Raider glanced at Doc, saw that he was raising his hands, then did the same.

Doc was looking at the young woman thoughtfully. She seemed to be in her late teens, and she had a lithe, almost boyish figure—it reminded him a little of those deer they'd seen bounding off a little while ago. Her skin was saddle-tan, and her large, dark eyes had a liquid, half-scared look to them. Under her loose cotton dress—cut along the lines of a flour sack—he could see the burgeoning shape of small but well-formed breasts just budding into maturity. That simple dress was all she wore; her legs and feet were bare.

"You want to put down that shotgun, young lady?" asked Doc.

The girl shook her head and waved the shotgun slightly to assure them that she still had it—and might use it.

"I'm guessing you can't speak," said Doc, still looking at her closely. "But you can read our lips, maybe—is that it?"

The girl nodded, but her expression remained wary.

"We're looking for Uriah," Doc continued. "We thought he'd be here, but we didn't expect to see you or anybody else here with him. My name's Doc and this is Raider."

That information only caused the girl to frown uncertainly; she kept the shotgun pointed.

"Goddamn it, miss, put that damned thing down," said Raider. "We can't stand here stupid like this all day."

The girl frowned and waggled the shotgun specifically at Raider for a moment.

Doc tried his hand at it. "Now look, young lady, we can understand why you're being careful. I can see that Uriah went off someplace, and I expect he told you to watch yourself if any strangers came around. But if we'd meant any harm, we wouldn't have come riding up here out in the open; we'd have snuck up on the place and you'd have never had a chance to grab that shotgun, let alone pointing it at us the way you're doing.''

Still frowning, the young woman tilted her head slightly to one side; there was still a touch of doubt in her expression, but not as much as she'd had a moment ago.

"Tell you what," drawled Raider. "I'm gonna walk your way. Nice and easy. And when I get to you, I'm goin' to stop right there; no sudden moves, no grabbin' for that shotgun of yours. All you gotta do then is relax and put it down, and then we can all be talkin' a little more friendly.''

As Doc glanced at him in disapproval, Raider, keeping his hands well away from his sides, and showing just a feathering of a smile, stepped forward and sauntered slowly toward the girl. Doc watched her eyes, as he was sure Raider must be doing. He guessed that if they flickered the wrong way, Raider would throw himself aside and try to avoid that shotgun blast, and while he admired his partner's courage in taking a risk like this, it wasn't one he himself would have taken.

The girl's face remained expressionless as Raider approached her. The shotgun, still leveled, did not sway or tremble in the slightest. Doc braced himself. If she did pull the trigger there would be a moment in which Doc could hurl himself forward and knock the weapon aside—while Raider either scrambled in the dirt or flew backward with a big hole in his belly. There had been times in the past when Doc had thought he might lose his partner for good, but on those occasions he'd been facing some very dangerous hombres and not a slip of a gal with the eyes of a startled doe.

Raider stopped about three feet from the muzzle of the shotgun. He kept his smile and spread his hands out even a littler farther away from him. "I don't think you want to shoot, gal. I don't think you got that mean a streak in you. Besides, it wouldn't do for Uriah to come back and find you'd blasted a couple of friends o' his all to hell, would it now?"

Still wary, the girl slowly raised the shotgun and swung it aside, although she was obviously ready to snap it into position again and pull the trigger at Raider's slightest move.

Raider stayed in place.

The girl dropped the stock of the shotgun to the ground and held it there, at her side.

Doc's shoulders rose and fell with his long sigh of relief.

"Now," said Raider, relaxing himself, "I expect we can have a friendly little visit, like Doc and I were figurin' on in the first place."

The girl both nodded and pointed at the cabin, and Raider and Doc turned and made their way to the door. Inside, there was a rough-hewn table with crude benches on either side of it, a large bed of crisscrossed rope on a frame in one corner, and the room's one finished piece of furniture, a rolltop desk, in another corner. Several seasoned alder logs burned gently in the big stone fireplace. On its hearth were several iron pots and a big black frying pan to show that it doubled as a cookstove. Near the fire, on an iron ring-stand that kept it just above the embers, sat a blue-enameled coffee pot with a wisp of steam dancing at its spout.

Doc was fascinated with the girl's expressiveness as she communicated with them wordlessly. She picked up the coffee pot, and, when she looked at them, her eyebrows seemed to form little question marks. They nodded, and in a moment she had them seated at the table with tin mugs of coffee in front of them. As they sipped it, burning their lips at first, she spun away briefly, then returned from the rolltop desk with a pencil and a sheaf of paper torn into small squares.

She sat at the table, scribbled, and shoved a square of

paper at them. On it she had written in a fine Spencerian hand, *My name is Tumbleweed.*

"Tumbleweed, huh?" said Raider. "Kinda fits, I'd say. You wouldn't be old Uriah's daughter or something like that, would you?"

She read his lips, shook her head, and began to scribble again. Several notes and several interjected questions later Doc and Raider understood much more about this half-wild little creature with her lithe, running deer's body and large, soft, half-scared eyes.

Uriah had given her her name. She'd had an Indian name before, and she knew its meaning—Dancing Bird—but, born a deaf mute, she'd never heard the sound of it and didn't know how to write it in phonetic English. She knew that the tribe in which she'd been raised was called "Ute" by white men, but that was not the name they gave themselves, which, in sign language, was expressed by the signs for "black" and "red."

Doc, still examining her features, was a little puzzled. "You don't exactly look Indian," he said.

Her quickly written notes explained that her father had been a white man—some long-forgotten trapper who had wandered into Ute territory—and that as a child she'd been treated contemptuously by the tribe because of this. She'd been forced to do menial work and had suffered beatings from the other women. Although many of the men forced her to submit to them when, with the first showing of blood, she became a woman, there was no hope that any would ever ask for her in marriage.

With nothing but a life of misery before her, she ran away one day. It was a long story how she'd wandered alone in greatest hardship across the rolling plains of the Great Basin and finally to these Colorado foothills, which the Utes still laid claim to. Eventually, half starving, she stumbled into a valley not far from here, and that was when Uriah Van Hawley found her and brought her to his cabin.

He had taught her to write. She in turn taught him sign language, and in this they now communicated fluently with each other. She cooked for him and kept his cabin clean. He was kind to her. She no longer wished to die.

"That there's quite a tale," said Raider. He was sipping his second cup of coffee, and Doc had a Virginia cheroot going. "If I was Uriah I'd sure admire havin' somebody as pretty as you here to come back to. Speakin' of which, just when do you expect him?"

Extending her hand, partly closed, she moved it back and forth and made the grasping motions that meant "hunting." Raider nodded. He'd communicated with enough Indians to have a smattering of sign language, which was the same with most tribes whatever their spoken language. Her next sign was to roll her hands as though they were blankets covering the earth, and that was the sign for "nightfall."

"He's out hunting," Raider translated for Doc. "Won't be back till dark."

"Don't know if we can wait that long," said Doc. He turned to Tumbleweed so she could see his lips moving. "Look, little gal, let me try to explain to you what we came here for and see if you can understand it. I don't know how much Uriah told you about the way things are in Tamarack Springs, but maybe you heard about Winfield Brent and how he nurses a pack of outlaws there."

Tumbleweed smiled and nodded to show that she knew.

"Raider and I," Doc continued, "have been sent to kinda clean things up. But before we can make a move, we have to know more about some of these outlaws holing up in the Springs. Uriah told me he's writing a history about them. Outside of Brent himself, Uriah probably knows better than any other man just who they all are, where they came from, and why they're here. If we could get a peek at some of the stuff he's been writing, it might tell us a little of what we need to know."

She glanced at the rolltop desk for a moment, then

looked at Doc and Raider again, frowning. She scribbled another note which said, *Uriah never shows his book to strangers*.

Doc nodded. "He said as much. But we ain't exactly strangers, and this is a special case. If Uriah were here, I'm sure he'd tell us what we want to know."

After a long moment of thought, Tumbleweed shook her head. She wrote on the scrap paper, *Sorry*, and showed the word to both of them.

Raider scowled. "Well, we ain't gonna force you or nothin'. We ain't that kind. But I sure wish you'd reconsider."

The girl switched her eyes back and forth across both of them as she obviously tried to make a decision. Suddenly she turned, found a key on a shelf, and went to the rolltop desk and opened it. Notebooks and loose sheaves of manuscript were inside, crammed into various spaces in disorderly fashion. Doc frowned. "This is gonna take some time. Tell you what. You and Raider visit awhile and I'll poke through all this and see what I can find."

Before long, Doc had become so immersed in his perusal of Uriah's writings that he was all but unaware of Raider and Tumbleweed, who sat at the table and kept each other company. In a dim way he realized that at first the girl was teaching Raider expressions in Indian sign language he hadn't yet learned; when they tired of this she brought out a chessboard, at which Raider shook his head and grumbled that chess was one game he'd never learned—first, because it went on forever and, second, because a man couldn't make any money at it. They settled for checkers, and Doc gathered from the way Raider cussed softly that the girl was beating him easily, game after game.

Borrowing a few scraps of paper, Doc made his own brief notes on the information he found: The names and criminal records of various lawbreakers who, following the Civil War, had committed crimes throughout the vast territory between Kansas City and San Francisco, and who, particularly, had visited Tamarack Springs at one time or another.

The time passed swiftly for Doc; Raider yawned and fidgeted as he lost one checker game after another and tried to pretend he didn't give a hoot about being beaten by the cheerful little half-breed girl. At last Doc felt he'd absorbed all he could in one sitting and signaled to Raider that he was ready to ride on back into town.

"Find anything?" asked Raider.

"Maybe," said Doc. "I'll tell you all about it on the way back."

The girl stood in front of the cabin and smiled and waved as they rode down the slope, turning several times in their saddles to wave back to her.

Now, as they crossed the rolling hills of buffalo grass between the town and the foothills of the mountain range, Raider seemed to be in one of his silent moods, and Doc had an idea he was still wondering how come he'd lost all those checker games to a mere slip of a gal. Far ahead they could see some of the buildings of Tamarack Springs, shimmering in the heat waves rising from the ground, faintly resembling a desert mirage. The landscape all around them was clear, with no cover for an ambush, and this enabled both of them to rest easy in their saddles as the horses plodded forward at a lazy walk.

A jackrabbit broke from cover and bounded off ahead of them. Making a lightning movement, Raider drew his .44 and dropped a bead on it.

Doc glanced at him. "They don't make good eating, Rade."

"I got no intention of shootin' the little bastard," Raider said gruffly. "Just keepin' in practice." He returned his weapon to its holster. Drawing it and aiming it, as he'd just done, seemed to bring him out of his silent mood. He shifted a little in the saddle to relieve the pressure on one buttock that might give him pins and needles on that side, then brought his horse forward so that it was more nearly abreast of Doc's mount. "Doc," he said, "you ain't told me a damn thing yet about what you found out back there."

"You didn't ask," said Doc.

Raider grunted to show he considered that beside the point.

"Well," said Doc, feeling now that he had the upper hand for the moment in their constant verbal game—though he wasn't quite sure why—"well, I went through most of that stuff of Uriah's in his rolltop desk, giving all those composition books of his a quick once-over and shuffling through all his notes. If he ever does get all of it into a book it's gonna be so big nobody can lift it. But I'll say this for it: He's got more about outlaws in that desk than there is in the Pinkerton files, or the Secret Service records, or anywhere else."

"Never mind all that," said Raider. "What did you learn?"

"At first," Doc said, "not much more than we already know. Mainly that Tamarack Springs has a sizable population of cutthroats and thieves, and that Uriah knows most of them by name, along with most of the crimes they've committed. I looked hard for somebody known to set fires, which might tell us who's doing Brent's dirty work, but I didn't come across anything helpful along those lines."

"Then what you're sayin' is you wasted your time."

"Hold on, Rade," said Doc. "I'm not finished yet. One of Uriah's stories was in a composition book all by itself and put aside, like it was special. It was about a big gold shipment that got itself lifted on the way from the Denver mint some years ago. In the late 'sixties, to be exact."

"That was before I had my first piece of ass," said Raider. "Did I ever tell you about it? There was this whore in Ft. Smith named Cora. She kept sayin', 'Christ, kid, put your legs on the *inside*—ain't you never been screwed before?' ''

"Shut up and listen, Rade. The Denver mint was established in 'sixty-two, when the government bought up a private mint a couple of dudes had opened there on account of all the gold that was being found at Cherry Creek and other nearby places. But the Union Pacific, when it got built, ran a hundred miles north, and Denver didn't get a railroad till 1870, when they built a spur down from Cheyenne—just like they're figuring to do now from Yancy to Tamarack Springs.''

"What the hell is this, a history lesson? You'll put me to sleep, Doc, like they used to in school.''

Doc ignored him and continued. "Before they got the railroad, the gold came in and the coins went out by wagon, like everything else. With a troop of soldiers guarding the shipment. But there was a man named William Flood who figured himself a way around that. He worked at the mint and knew all about the shipments that were planned. On this occasion he substituted an exact duplicate of one of the wagons and spirited away the real one. It took lots of maneuvering, like in a crooked three-card monte game, but he got it done. They didn't discover they had one wagon full of lead pigs instead of gold coins till they got to Cheyenne four days later. By that time William Flood had flown the coop, and it even took them a while afterward to figure out he was the one. Which gave him a good head start. And there wasn't a clue which way he'd gone. With almost a million dollars in gold. About the biggest robbery anybody ever made.''

"Wouldn't mind pullin' off one like that myself,'' said Raider dryly, "if I wasn't so law-abidin'.''

"Well, to make a long story short,'' said Doc—

"Which you ain't doin','' said Raider—

"To make a long story short,'' Doc repeated, "they picked up this William Flood in San Francisco maybe a year later when he tried to spend some of the coins, which had a special mark on them so they could be identified. They were the last ones out of a mold that got destroyed to make way for the new coins. Flood got sent to the hoosegow. In fact, it was the Pinkerton Agency that helped bring him to justice, so all this is somewhere in the files in Chicago if you want to look it up there.''

"If we ever get to Chicago. The way old Allan keeps us jumpin' around, I got an idea he don't ever want to see us.''

"Just listen, will you? I'm not through yet. They never did recover most of what Flood stole. He just plumb wouldn't tell them where he'd cached it, though they tried hard to find out. They had no idea where he'd been from the time he rode off with the gold till the time he popped up in San Francisco. But Uriah Van Hawley, according to his notes, knows at least one place Flood drifted into while he was on the owl hoot. And that place was Tamarack Springs.''

"How come Uriah knows this?''

"I'm not sure. He drew a line under it, like it was important. And he wrote himself another little note in the margin. 'Gold cached in T.S.?' He must've had reason to think it might be.''

Raider, no longer bored with Doc's discourse, was frowning now as he turned this information over in his mind. "So maybe there's a fortune in gold buried somewhere around here. And maybe there's more than one person lookin' for it. Brent, for example. With that much at stake, it'd pay him to wait for years and go to a lot of trouble to keep the outlaws comin' in—hopin' someday one of 'em might know where the gold is and lead him to it. This would explain some of the queersome things he's been doin'.''

"Exactly," said Doc. "Might even be he's waiting for this William Flood himself to show up.''

"When's Flood supposed to get out of the hoosegow?''

"I don't know. But the home office would. All the

more reason for me to ride down to Yancy and send a telegraph. Also, we've got to get hold of Uriah in person and find out what else he knows. Looks like we've got some busy days ahead.''

''Looks like,'' said Raider. He turned his frown straight ahead, and they continued to ride in silence for several minutes.

They could see the buildings of the town more clearly now. They were no longer in the haze of rising heat that, a short time before, had made them shimmer like a mirage. At first, the column of smoke was too small to catch their attention—it could have been rising from a chimney or even a small trash fire. But as they watched, it grew, and within minutes a fat gray cloud was billowing up into the air above the town.

Realization came to both men simultaneously. In the same moment, they looked at each other sharply, and Raider said, ''That there's another building burning!''

''I believe it is,'' said Doc mildly.

Both men heeled their horses hard and headed for the town at a hungry gallop.

CHAPTER ELEVEN

Everyone in sight was so busy running around, shouting, staring, stumbling over other folks, that scarcely anyone noticed Doc and Raider as they rode upon the scene.

The center of the scene was the schoolhouse, which lay just outside the town proper, and which was now crackling with leaping flames that were sending the rolling gray smoke high in the air. As they neared the heat of the conflagration, it parched their cheeks and the acrid smell of the smoke was bitter in their nostrils. All around, the horses that had been brought to the spot were fidgeting and rearing, their eyes rolling with terror. In the schoolhouse, which was rapidly becoming a shell, the flames sounded with a soft, stuttering roar.

"That there," said Raider staring, "is just plain a patch of hell itself!"

"An excellent description," said Doc, as Raider glanced at him, sensing sarcasm but unable to put his finger on it.

A short distance away from the burning structure was the new fire engine with its bright red paint and gilded curlicues. Smoke and steam poured from the top of its boiler in pulsations, as it might from a locomotive, and the wheels and pistons that linked the steam engine to the pumping mechanism were spinning and churning. An intake hose of gutta percha and canvas ran from the engine to a huge trough of water on a separate wagon bed that because of its great weight had been dragged here by another four-horse team. All the horses had been unhitched from both vehicles and shunted off to the side.

Ab Ormsby, in full uniform, was standing at the driver's seat of the engine, waving his arms and shouting commands that nobody seemed to hear in all the commotion. Armand Sirois, his immensely fat body covered by a linen duster, was crouched in the back of the engine, by the pumping mechanism, where he seemed to be working frantically at its valves.

In a moment, Doc and Raider understood why the Frenchman was fumbling and sweating. Between the fire engine and the blazing structure two men stood holding the long brass nozzle of the hose. The water was emerging from it in a thin, weak stream that scarcely reached the edge of the fire; obviously, the withering heat kept them from bringing it any closer.

Raider scowled at the sorry attempt. "They'd do better just pissin' on it!" he said in disgust mingled with a touch of surprise. "That there machine ain't worth a damn!"

Fire Chief Ormsby had evidently come to the same conclusion. He had organized and was directing a bucket line of a dozen men from the water cart to the fire. The man at the cart would keep dipping buckets and passing them along, while the others, standing abreast, would relay them toward the fire, working cross-handed to bring the empty buckets back to the source of water for refilling. The last man in line would toss the contents of each bucket, as he received it, toward the fire. Most of the time, Doc noticed, the water didn't even reach it.

Although Doc and Raider both had plenty of criticism in their craws, there was nothing to be gained by airing it now. Both men sprang forward to lend a hand at the bucket line.

The roof had long since caved in, and now, with everything inside the structure disintegrated in a white-hot glow, the walls caught fire and crumpled before everyone's eyes, sparks and embers spitting out as they fell. With not much left to fuel the fire, the heat became less fearsome, enabling the hose men and the bucketeers to press at least a few yards closer, though they still weren't near enough to get much water on the blaze.

Like everyone else on hand, Doc and Raider lost track of time, but they guessed it to be almost an hour later before the flames stopped leaping. By that time what had been the schoolhouse was a pile of blackened rubble. The bucketeers were able to move in closer to this and toss water on the embers, making them steam and sizzle.

The crowd, which must have included nearly everyone in town, continued to mill about, breaking up into small groups engaged in heated argument and speculation. Doc and Raider stalked toward Armand Sirois, who was still turning valves and pushing levers on the engine.

Sirois looked up as they approached. His round face glistened with sweat that looked like melted grease. His rosebud lips were tightly pursed and his eyes were glossy as tears of frustration tried to form themselves within them.

"Goddamn it," said Raider, "what the hell happened?"

"It was a bullet!" he said. "*Sacre bleu*—that is the only answer!"

"What bullet?"

"You see here?" Sirois pointed to the pump housing. "It was struck when those brigands attacked the train! The cap had not been affixed and the inside of the pump was exposed. Here in the heart of my beautiful machine! It has suffered a mortal blow!"

"You mean she's busted for good?"

"Only a new *coquille* will make her well—and the nearest one is in France!"

"A new what?"

"*Coquille*. Shell. The part is not a shell, of course, but

it resembles the spiral of certain seashells, so that is what I call it. In English I believe one would say the impeller.''

"I never heard tell of it in either language," said Raider, "but I think I can understand the sad news you're gettin' at. That fire engine of yours, as she sits here now, ain't worth a rat's ass.''

Sirois nodded and sighed deeply. "You have reason, Monsieur Raid-air,'' he said.

Night had fallen before the last ember in the rubble of the schoolhouse stopped glowing, but there were still embers of excitement throughtout the town. It was safe to say that the fire was the principal topic of conversation at every dinner table in Tamarack Springs that evening.

At the boardinghouse, Ma Ormsby served chicken and dumplings, while Ab related in great detail how he and Sirois, at the firehouse, had responded to the alarm, how he'd sent men to round up the volunteers, and how he'd rushed to hitch horses to the engine and water wagon before clattering off to the fire itself.

"Then, when we got there," he growled, wiping gravy from his Lincoln beard, "all she'd do was give out that tiny squirt.''

Doc was sitting next to Heather this evening. She was feeling the lump in his left trouser leg under the table, and he had been trying to keep a straight face all along. He turned this straight face toward Ab now and said, "How come you didn't know it was busted? Didn't you test it beforehand?''

"We was just about to," said Ab sadly. "You see, all the parts wasn't put together, so they wouldn't get damaged in shipment, and Sirois, he's been busy gettin' 'em all in place ever since the engine got here. With them fat fingers of his, he don't work too fast. And besides, he was mostly busy talkin', explaining the whole damn thing to me so's I'd know all about it.''

"Then you understand how that bullet knocked out the

contraption. Damaged this 'seashell,' or whatever the Frenchman calls it.''

"The impeller," Ormsby said, nodding. "Got it right here." He rose long enough to step to his jacket, which hung on a clothes tree in the other room, and bring back a brass object, maybe the size of a small apple, that did indeed resemble a certain kind of spiral seashell. "Up to now," he said, "there's been two kinds of pumps: piston, like Ma's got for water here in the kitchen, and rotary, which is kind of a paddlewheel. Sirois has come up with this centrifugal pump, which throws a lot more water a lot faster. With the old kind we could only use hoses up to maybe an inch in diameter at the most, but with the seashell pump we can toss a stream that'd knock a bull on his ass—''

"Abner!" said Ma, looking stern.

"—a bull on his side," Ormsby amended, "at more'n a hundred feet. Now, this one here ain't the main pump. But the centrifugal pump has to keep gettin' primed, and that's its only disadvantage. There's a whole bunch o' valves that work automatic to exhaust air from the intake hoses and keep the water flowing. This here baby impeller takes care of the priming, which ain't much of a job, but the rest of the pump just won't work without it.''

Doc took the part and turned it over and over in his hand, studying it. "Yes. I can see how it works. The impeller spins, and the water spirals through it, picking up speed. Mighty interesting. I've always wanted to be an engineer, you know.''

"Doc," Raider said sourly, "you always wanted to be everything.''

Doc ignored him and continued. "Right here," he said, touching a place where the spiral fin was distorted, "is where the bullet hit. And that, of course, is where the passage of the water is blocked.''

"Fancy talk, Doc," said Raider. "But all you're sayin'

is what we already know. Which is, the damn thing just won't work."

"True enough," said Doc, unabashed. "And I expect it might take two or three months for Monsieur Sirois to send back to France for a new one. A lot of buildings could burn down by then."

"Could—and maybe will," said Ormsby, his frown deepening. "I got a look at them ashes after everybody left. That schoolhouse fire was set, same as the others."

Doc reached down under the table and gently removed Heather's hand from his crotch so that he could concentrate. "How do you know, Ab?" he asked, trying to make it sound casual.

"There's lots o' ways you can tell," Ormsby said, "when you know what to look for. Mainly, when somebody starts a fire he gets it goin' good and hard in one place with somethin' like coal oil, and that always leaves traces. Natural fires just kind of grow from some little blaze somewhere—in fact, with them, you usually can't find where they started. And when it comes to the schoolhouse, there's one more thing. There was nothin' in it that would start a fire accidental-like; even the potbelly stove they use in the winter was all shut up for the season."

Still looking thoughtful, Doc nodded and said, "I see. Ab, you mind if I take that seashell thing and hold on to it a bit?"

"What for?"

"Just want to study it."

Ab shrugged and said, "Go ahead, Doc. It ain't no good to us the way it is."

Ma Ormsby and Heather now rose and began to clear the table. Ma glanced at Doc and Raider. "I forgot to tell you boys—come Saturday night you'll have to make do for yourselves. I'll leave some beans or something and you can heat them on the stove. Hope you don't mind."

"Don't mind at all, ma'am," said Raider. "We won't be here for dinner anyway on Saturday. Rina Larkin's throwin' a big party out at the XL, and we got ourselves invited."

Ma looked surprised. "Why, that's where *I'll* be," she said. "Cooking for that party."

"Rina's called her in before," Ab explained, "for them parties of hers. Ain't nobody can whip up a fancy, full-course dinner the way Ma can; in Chicago she used to do it for all them meat-packin' millionaires. Myself, I don't care too much for 'em 'cause they always give you too many forks and you never know which one to use. The chow's mighty fine, though—I'll say that much."

Ma laughed. "Ab can't enjoy it 'less he ties his napkin under his chin and scoops up the peas with his knife. And you ought to hear him eat soup. Sounds like a brass band out of tune."

"Ma," said Ab, returning her laugh, "you been tryin' to make me over for close to thirty years. If I was you, I'd give up." He addressed Doc and Raider again. "She's still the best cook west o' the Mississippi, and maybe a good patch east of it too. She's gonna win first prize again come the Statehood Celebration—and that there's gonna be a *real* party."

"Been meaning to ask you about that," said Doc. "Rade and I saw the posters around town, but we've been too busy to find out more."

Ab Ormsby began to stuff his corncob pipe with dark tobacco from a small buckskin sack. "Colorado was admitted to the Union August 1, 1876, and we celebrate that every year here in the Springs. Gives us a good excuse to have a fair and reminds everybody how the town's gonna grow. We put on a rodeo, and the ranchers show off their prize stock so the judges can award ribbons. There's prizes for the womenfolk, too: best pie, best pickles, and best recipe, which Ma always wins. Heather here is gonna be in the kissin' booth, where the best-lookin' gals in town put out kisses for two bits apiece—proceeds to the church.

It's a real, rip-roarin' celebration, and I expect you boys are gonna enjoy it.''

"It's rip-roaring, all right," Ma said with a frown of disapproval. "Half the men in town get themselves pie-eyed drunk. Just once I'd like to see a fair without all those fights breaking out and all those six-guns going off in the air."

"Got to have a little good, clean fun," said Ab, chuckling. "Wouldn't be the same without it."

"At any rate," said Ma, "I'm sure that Mr. Raider, and Doc Weatherbee, who used to be a preacher, will be behaving themselves properly."

"You can count on it, ma'am," said Doc piously.

Raider threw a disgusted glance at him, but Doc's expression remained quite bland.

Most of the light and all of the noise to be found on the main street of Tamarack Springs at this hour was in the vicinity of the Grand Palace saloon. Doc and Raider strolled on the board sidewalk some distance down the street from that establishment, with the night air cool on their cheeks. They'd walked into town from the boardinghouse, though Raider, who had the habit of forking his horse just to cross the street, had wanted to ride. "The walk'll do us good," Doc had said. "Loosens up the limbs and cleanses the bodily humors."

"What the hell are bodily humors, anyway?" Raider asked. "Everybody's always talkin' about them, but nobody can say just what they are."

"That's because for someone not versed in medicine, they're difficult to explain."

"Bullshit," said Raider. "But if you're so set on walkin', we'll walk."

Now, as they came to a small alleyway, Doc halted, peered for a moment, then turned into it. "From what Ab said, it must be down this way."

"What must be down this way?" Raider asked, looking at Doc sharply.

"Sam Ruby's place. I've got some business with Sam. Guess I forgot to tell you."

"Like hell you forgot to tell me. You're playin' that game o' yours again. The one where you get all mysterious, so I end up askin' a bunch o' questions and soundin' like a damn fool. All right, Doc, what's it all about this time?"

"You'll see," said Doc.

Raider snorted.

A short distance down the narrow side street was a small house that was little more than a shack. Over its front door, on a protruding bar, hung three gilded wooden balls, and below them a sign that said S. RUBY, JEWELER & PAWN-BROKER. Light showed through a pair of curtains drawn across the front window.

Doc knocked, and a moment later the door opened. Sam Ruby looked up at them with his restless, quizzical eyes. He was again in a collarless shirt, and a pair of narrow, steel-rimmed glasses rested near the tip of his broad, stubby nose. "*Shalom*, Weatherbee!" he said, seeing Doc. "I was wondering if you'd drop around, already. It so happens I've got a chessboard already set up inside. I've been practicing."

"I'm not surprised to hear it, the way you play," said Doc. "But this isn't a social call."

Sam shrugged. "So, it's business. Well, for a fellow chess player I'm always open for business. Please. Come inside."

Sam's shop consisted of a small room in front and a door in back leading to what was probably his living quarters. Under a glass counter near the front door a few pieces of jewelry—mostly rings, bracelets, and necklaces of silver and pewter—had been laid out on a black cloth, and on the walls hung several guns, guitars, and silver-studded bridles that had evidently been pawned with him.

On one long shelf rested a motley collection of objects, ranging from a cuckoo clock to an under-the-bed night potty of fine porcelain with roses and gold-leaf curlicues painted upon it.

Behind the counter was a small table with chairs around it. A chessboard with the men in place had been set up here. Sam led the way and said, "Sit down, gentlemen. Sit down, already. If we're going to talk business, we might as well be comfortable."

As Doc took a chair he glanced at the rear of the room and saw a workbench with a small vise clamped to its edge and with various tools hooked to the backboard behind it. He nodded to himself when he saw this, and Raider, seeing him nod, scowled to show that he still wondered what in hell his partner was up to.

"Well, Sam," said Doc, "what I've got in mind is this."

Sam put a hand up to halt him. "The business can wait. I don't get many visitors, and this is a chance, already, to enjoy a little conversation. Sit right where you are, gentlemen. We will all have a glass of tea."

"A glass of *tea*?" said Raider, bringing his head up.

"As we drink it in the old country," said Sam. "I will show you."

He busied himself for a moment at a small charcoal stove in the corner, where a kettle was steaming, and then, on a tray, brought tumblers of reddish-brown liquid to the table. Beside the glasses was a long string of rock candy.

"Like this," said Sam, sitting down. He broke off one of the sugar crystals, put it between his teeth, and then, lifting the glass with his palm underneath it so that his fingers wouldn't burn, he sipped the hot brew through the sugar. "I couldn't tell you why, but it always tastes better this way," he said.

Doc and Raider drank the tea as Sam had, but they also glanced quickly at each other to agree silently that it was far from the best beverage they'd ever tasted.

"The tea reminds me of home, you see," said Sam. "And, out here in the West, every once in a while homesick I get."

"What brought you to these parts, anyway?" asked Doc.

Sam shrugged and spread his hands. "Such a long story. It would put you to sleep. I'll tell it, anyway. You heard, maybe, about King Midas, who, everything he touched, it turned to gold? Well, you are looking at the opposite of King Midas. Everything I touch turns to manure. It's been that way ever since I can remember."

Doc had to smile. "Maybe you got a curse on you from some Indian medicine man. They can do some strange things."

Sam shook his head. "It was before I even came west. Everything going wrong. My business, my love life, my digestion, even my chess game. I looked all around me and decided it must be the big city—though it shouldn't have been."

"Why not? Cities can make a man feel trapped," said Raider.

"Not a man who was born to live in one," said Sam. "For centuries, our people have congregated in the cities, and it is there we have learned to survive. It has made us what we are: merchants and money changers, or a lucky few who become scholars, doctors, lawyers. Not many are trappers, explorers, ranchers—men who work under the sky. *Selah!* That is the way things are. But . . ."

He paused for so long that Doc said, "But what?"

"But there was a time," continued Sam, "when we wandered the desert, like nomads, looking at the endless horizons and the land stretching away on all sides as far as a man could see, and maybe some of that is in my blood somewhere. One day I just knew I wouldn't be happy until I pushed west, where a man wasn't crowded and could make a new start. That day I picked up and left. And here I am."

"Good," said Doc. "Glad you're feeling better."

"Feeling better?" Sam Ruby sighed deeply. "I'm as miserable as I ever was. Now, what brings you gentlemen here?"

Doc reached into the pocket of his pearl-gray jacket, took out the cockleshell part from the fire engine, and dropped it on the table. "Ever see anything like this before, Sam?"

Sam stepped to the workbench, found a jeweler's loupe, screwed it into one eye, and examined the object under its magnification. "Some kind of pendant? It's not gold, if that's what you thought. Pure brass. Worth a few dollars, maybe—but who would buy it?"

"We didn't come to pawn this, Sam," said Doc. "It's from the new fire engine, which won't work without it. You can see where those spiraling fins are all mashed and bent out of place. We thought maybe you could fix it."

"Fix it?" He continued to squint at the part, turning it this way and that. "I can see how these grooves are supposed to be, but reshaping them wouldn't be easy. Brass is a lot harder to work than gold or silver." He took the jeweler's loupe from his eye and put the impeller down on the table again. "I am sorry to say, gentlemen, that repairing this would be impossible."

Doc rose. "Well, if you can't, you can't. Guess we'll just have to wait till a new one gets here, all the way from France."

"Why do that?" asked Sam. "I'll try to fix this one."

"You just said it was impossible."

"Of course I did. That way, if I can't fix it I've already got my excuse. If I can, you realize it's a miracle. Either way I haven't hurt my reputation."

"Sam," said Raider, "you're as hard to follow as a fox in a bramble bush."

"I know," said Sam Ruby, grinning. "It's how I keep from getting skinned."

CHAPTER TWELVE

Raider wasn't sure which irritated him more—the polite nonsense talk at the big dining table or the way Doc took part in it, smiling as though he was actually enjoying it.

Everybody sat in Xavierina Larkin's big dining room, with food piled on fancy gilt-edged China covering the table, and with Mexican servants in white coats gliding in and out of the kitchen bringing one course after another. There were almost twenty guests, most of them what Raider supposed would be called the leading lights of the town. He'd been introduced to everybody from the mayor on down, but most of the names had been mumbled, so that by now he'd forgotten them.

Aside from all that, Raider had a difficult decision to make. Every once in a while Rina, presiding at the head of the table, would glance his way and a barely noticeable smile would twitch at her full, red lips. It was clear enough what she was saying: Be patient, Raider; wait till everyone's gone. But Claudette Sirois, who sat beside her fat husband, was glancing at him too. That little beauty mark on her chin, and the thin black velvet ribbon around her neck, helped to make her glances both mischievous and provocative. What she was saying was that if Raider would quietly follow them to the hotel after the party she'd slip away as soon as her husband began to snore—which shouldn't take too long.

Monsieur Sirois was in his element. He wore a starched wing collar and a broad blue ribbon—an honor of some kind bestowed upon him by the Third Republic—across the billowing expanse of his chest and stomach. He held up a glass of the wine Rina had served. "My congratulations, Madame!" he said to her. "A true Medoc of the grand class! I did not expect to find anything like it here, so far from civilization. It does much to make my long and arduous journey worthwhile."

Raider whispered to Doc, "The damn stuff tastes like grape juice gone a little sour to me."

"Pretend you like it," Doc whispered back. "Don't spoil the party."

After dinner, everybody retired to the big main room, where brandy was served as they sat around like lumps on a log. Rina stood before the group and cleared her throat. "Now that we're all here, ladies and gentlemen," she said, "it's as good as a meeting. And there has been a development you should all know about."

She waved a letter in the air, then opened it.

"I have just received this from our lawyers in Denver. As you know, they are watching things closely there, and they know about all the decisions the railroad is making. It seems that the Denver & Rio Grande is now having second thoughts about building that spur up from Yancy. I'm afraid our reputation as a haven for outlaws is just a little too much for them. They're not so sure now that we can make Tamarack Springs into a prosperous cattle center so that they'd realize a return on their investment."

Ab Ormsby took his unlighted corncob pipe from his mouth. "It's what we've been sayin' all along, Rina. We got to get rid o' them polecats. Thing to do is arrest every one of 'em and turn 'em over to the authorities who want 'em. We've had this unwritten law that they can stick around as long as they don't make trouble here, and in some ways that's been good for the town. We ain't had a bank robbery yet, for example. But times are changin'. We better start usin' our written laws, like any respectable town, I'm thinkin'."

"Unfortunately," continued Rina, "our marshal, Dan Carver, seems to be on Brent Winfield's side. Up to now we haven't fired him because there just wasn't anybody else handy enough with a gun to keep all these lawbreakers under control. Well, I think we've finally got somebody on hand who'd be able to do it."

"Who might that be?" asked Ormsby.

All eyes followed Rina's glance as it settled on Raider. "Mr. Raider here," she said.

Raider looked up. "Who, me?"

"You, Raider," said Rina. "I'm proposing that the council takes a vote to appoint you town marshal. I'm sure your partner, Doc Weatherbee here, can find another assistant."

"You left somethin' out," said Raider.

"What?"

"You didn't ask *me* yet."

"Very well. I'm asking you. Will you accept?"

"Can't say right now," said Raider, frowning. "Something like this, Doc and I better talk it over."

"Then please do. You should be quite comfortable in the music room. We'll continue our meeting here."

The music room was across the main hallway—in effect a small parlor with an upright piano against the wall. Doc sat down at this and began to pick out "Yankee Doodle" with one finger.

"We're supposed to talk, not rehearse for a damn concert," said Raider.

"You know something about 'Yankee Doodle'?" asked Doc. "General Grant once said he only knew two tunes. One was 'Yankee Doodle' and the other was not."

"Then General Grant and I are more alike than I

thought,'' drawled Raider. ''Doc, you're hemmin' and hawin' again. You can't think of what to say.''

''That's right,'' said Doc, still poking at the keys. ''On the one hand it might help us out if you get to be town marshal; on the other hand it might just lead to complications. The home office didn't plan on us sticking around here long enough for you to take a marshal's job. In fact, they must be wondering why we haven't finished our little routine investigation by now.''

''Maybe so,'' said Raider. ''But it looks like we got more than a routine investigation on our hands. I'm thinkin' about all that gold that's supposed to be buried somewheres around here. If we could recover that, it'd be bigger than the seven hundred thousand old Alan got back from that Adams Express robbery in 'sixty-six. And, by his own regulations, operatives get five percent of any loot they recover. He'll squeal like a stuck pig, but he'll have to pay it.''

''Now, let's look at this whole thing a little more carefully,'' said Doc. He hit a wrong note, winced, and tried again. ''You get to be marshal, Dan Carver'll be out on his ass, and he won't like it. Neither will Brent. You'll have guns looking for you on all sides.''

''I can take care of myself,'' growled Raider.

''I know that, but a smart gambler doesn't push his luck. Rade, now that I think it over, I believe you better tender the widow Larkin your regrets. Better yet—put it off. They all might think it just a little strange if you say no flat on the barrelhead. Tell 'em you'll decide in a day or two. That'll give us time to ride on down to Yancy and have a little confab with the Denver office on the telegraph wire.''

Raider was thoughtful for a long moment. ''Hate to say it, Doc, but I think you're right this time. Now, will you do me a favor?''

''What?''

''Stop playin' that goddamn piano so we can get back where the whiskey is.''

• • •

The rambling main house of the XL ranch lay quiet in the moonlight. The guests, with one exception, had departed long ago on their horses and in their buggies, thanking Rina at the door for what they all agreed had been a right fine dinner party—Tamarack Springs needed more genteel, civilized affairs like this, and, by God, one of these days it would have them.

There was only one light showing in the house now. It glowed softly through the curtains of Xavierina Larkin's bedroom in the rear.

Raider sat on the edge of the four-poster bed within. It was about the softest bed he'd ever sat on, including those they had in that Chicago sporting house where you could get any color of girl you wanted. His clothes were piled on a brocaded chair in another corner of the room, and he sat naked, just a little uncomfortable at the way he smelled, which was very sweet and somehow not manly.

That was on account of the perfumed soap in Rina's bath. It had been waiting, the long tub filled with warm water, in a smaller, adjoining room, and she'd insisted that he use it first. After he'd done so and returned to the bedroom wrapped in a huge towel, Rina had taken her turn, and she was in there now. Raider had not had so much as a glimpse of the servants who must have brought the buckets to fill and empty the tub, though he doubted his presence was unknown to them.

Raider was beginning to fidget when Rina at last reentered the room. She was wearing a pinkish robe of almost transparent silk, its collar piped with ostrich feathers. The full, rounded outlines of her figure were completely visible under it, and Raider reflected that here was a woman who didn't need hoopskirts or bustles to make her look like a woman. As she came toward him, her eyes intent and even greedy upon him, she loosened the sash of the robe and it came apart in front to reveal the rolling hills and valleys of her body: Two great breasts so expansive that there was only a tight seam between them, a waist drawn tightly in as though by a purse string, and a delightful shallow dome of a belly below it, ballasted by a soft patch of dark beaver fur.

Raider stood, and, as he did, his member rose like the arm of a giant crane until it stood there at an angle, pointed at the upper torso of the woman gliding toward him.

Rina halted three feet before him and slipped the robe away from her broad shoulders, letting it fall to the floor. The smile on her full, red lips was knowing and confident, as though to say there would now be a ceremony in which she knew every word, every movement.

"Tonight," said Rina, in her low, purring voice, "I am going to show you pleasures you never knew existed."

"I doubt you will," said Raider, smiling, "but I sure don't mind your tryin'."

She closed the remaining distance between them, and, reaching down to grab Raider's great, upright rod, she pressed him down upon the bed and clambered on top of him. She then rolled both of them around until Raider, resting on his hands and knees, was astride her. She shuffled her body downward until his rod lay between the immense globes of her breasts. She placed her hands on the sides of her breasts and squeezed upward.

"Start pumping, Raider," she whispered, her eyes beginning to roll with her own feeling of pleasure. "A little here, and then a little somewhere else."

As he slid his poleax back and forth between the huge globes, her tongue flickered out to tease the end of it when it neared her with each stroke.

It was, Raider soon discovered, only the beginning. Writhing and squirming, Rina twisted herself into so many positions that Raider lost count (though he was not really counting), and with each she found a new crevice to take his thick, throbbing staff. She received it under her arms, in the crook of her elbow, between her thighs, in the bend of her knees, and in the crack of her swelling buttocks. When she was ready to mouth it, she slipped to a sitting position on the floor, her back against the bed, and had him spread-eagle himself over her as she swallowed almost half of it, all the while holding his balls and hefting them gently, like bags of lead shot. Her tongue worked furiously upon its rubbery surface, and Raider had all he could do to hold himself in.

"And now the final place," she said, climbing into the bed again.

The final position was nothing new to Raider; it was the way it was usually done. But he was so inflamed now by all the variations she'd put him through that their conventional coupling seemed, in its intensity, like something he'd never experienced before. It was her response that made it extraordinary. She met each of his thrusts with a counterthrust, her entire, curvaceous body in constant motion in a series of quivering spasms, her face contorted with pleasure as she rolled her head back and forth, moaning in ecstasy.

There was, at last, the ultimate thrust as he forced every inch of himself into her and then exploded. She wailed with the joy of it and held his body crushed to hers as he continued to throb within her.

Doc had always said he kind of liked the time in between, when you were resting, getting ready for the next one, and maybe he was right, Raider decided; there *was* a quiet pleasure in it, though it didn't compare to the actual excitement of doing something. Rina, stretched out beside him, gave off her body warmth and the musky odor of that perfumed soap of hers. She ran her fingers lightly through the hair on Raider's chest.

"Raider," she said, "you're more man than any I ever knew, with the possible exception of my late husband, Ben. And I'll wager I'm more woman than you ever had before."

"No complaints," said Raider, with a slight smile.

"We'd do well together, Raider. Not just here, in bed. You're hard, and a little mean, and so am I. You can take care of yourself. Standing off those men of Brent's—all six of them—three times in a row. Every one of them gunhands. Even when they tried to ambush you at night, they couldn't—which might have been luck, but a man like you makes his own luck."

"If you're makin' compliments," said Raider, "I guess I'm supposed to thank you. I'll have to ask Doc. He's the one knows all about sociable talk."

Rina laughed. "These aren't just empty compliments, Raider. They're leading up to what I'm thinking. About you and me. We'd make a good combination. We could end up owning the town. And the town would be only the beginning."

"If you're sayin' what I think you are," said Raider cautiously, "I'm not ready yet to be corralled. Maybe never will be."

"I can see that. Ben had the horizon in his eyes before I made him look down and pay attention to what was under his nose. After that, he made his fortune. I can do the same for you."

"Maybe." Raider was frowning deeply.

"Hear me out," she said. "I want you to take that marshal's job, Raider, and keep it till Winfield Brent's out of the way, so we can start building up this town together. Do it right, and I'm all yours, along with the XL and a small fortune we can grow into a huge fortune. The town? The whole state, perhaps, one of these days. Or more. The sky's the limit."

"That there's quite a dream, Rina," he said noncommittally.

"Do you realize what I'm offering?" she persisted. "Do you know how many men come sniffing around here like coyotes, trying to get it? There are some in town who'd dump their wives and children if I smiled at them the right way. Dan Carver, the marshal, has looked at me, hungry, and so has Winfield Brent. Even Clay Dillard, my foreman, only stays on here because he thinks he has a chance. I have to put him off all the time. Think about it, Raider. A fortune and the best lovemaking you'll ever find, whenever you want it, which I suspect will be all the time. What more could a man ask?''

"I'll think about it," said Raider. "But not now. Right now, we both got better things to do than think.''

He rolled to his side and pulled her well-upholstered body, all woman and then some, hard against his own.

CHAPTER THIRTEEN

As always at noon, when the sun was hot and high, the dusty main street of Tamarack Springs had a stillness to it. Doc and Raider, strolling side by side at a leisurely pace, saw little movement ahead or on either side, except perhaps for a dog who scuttled into an alley, or a big black crow that was pecking at the remains of a dead cat near the edge of town. It flew off clumsily, and not really scared, as they approached. When they had passed it, the crow returned to its meal again.

A few horses stood at hitching rails, switching at flies with their tails. Through the glass windows of the storefronts they could occasionally see people moving in the cooler darkness within. A Mexican slept with his back to the wall and a sombrero over his eyes in front of the dry-goods emporium, and a Navaho squatted near the general store, the jewelry he had for sale on a small blanket in front of him; but they were both so motionless that they seemed inanimate objects set in place to round out the quiet tableau, like figures in a wax museum.

Raider increased his pace, and Doc said quietly, "Slow down, Rade. We've got to look like we're not going anywhere."

"I know that," growled Raider. "But if we were goin' any slower, we'd be walkin' backward."

"How many times do we have to go over it again?"
Doc asked, irritated. "A hundred to one, we're being
watched—Brent still doesn't know just what to make of
us. We can't ride to Yancy without the telegraph key, and
that's in the wagon, and the wagon's at the livery stable.
No way to sneak up to it, so we have to go through the
town."

"Doc, you sure have a way of sayin' everything ten
times. You're gonna run out of breath one o' these days."

They had not greeted each other until late this Sunday
morning. The Ormsbys were already off to church when
Raider rode in quietly from the XL after spending the night
with Rina. He was well satisfied, not so much exhausted
as relaxed into a kind of half sleepiness, and when he
found Doc in much the same state he knew that Heather
must have come to his bed in the darkness, slipping away
just before dawn.

Doc sighed. "Never thought I'd say it, but I'm glad
we're riding out. I could use a night all to myself for a
change."

"Speak for yourself, Doc," said Raider. "By this evening I'm gonna be as horny as ever."

"Well, hold on to yourself," said Doc. "We've got
business to take care of. And remember what we say in
case we do get noticed riding south. We're expecting a
shipment of medicines on the train, and that's why we're
heading for Yancy."

"You do the bullshitting, Doc," said Raider with a
slight grin. "You're good at it."

They were nearly abreast of the Grand Palace hotel and
saloon by now, and it seemed as quiet as all the other
establishments, though the horses in front of it showed that
there were at least a few early drinkers inside.

Suddenly there was a burst of motion in all the stillness
as a figure emerged from the swinging doors of the saloon,
stepping forward and coming to a halt at the edge of the
porchlike board sidewalk. It was Clay Dillard, Rina Larkin's

foreman. He was in his usual dusty cowhand's garb, and his sun-reddened face was turned toward Doc and Raider. At this distance they couldn't see his pale eyes clearly, but there was not much doubt that they were fastened upon them. They did not fail to notice that Dillard's gun was tied snugly to his thigh with a length of rawhide, and that his right hand was hooked off to one side, not too far from it.

Neither Doc nor Raider changed pace. Keeping his own eyes straight ahead, Raider said quietly, "Looks like Dillard's got somethin' in mind."

"Damn his ass if he does," said Doc. "The last thing we want right now is to be noticed."

Dillard stepped down into the dust. He turned toward Doc and Raider and slowly began walking toward them. He kept his head still and his eyes riveted upon them.

"Somethin' tells me we just ain't goin' to get past Mr. Dillard," drawled Raider.

Doc and Raider halted.

Dillard came forward a little more, until they could see his pale eyes and the hostile glare that was in them, and his scraggly blond hair, hanging down in tassels from his trailworn hat to his shoulders. His slim, loose-jointed build was like that of a mountain lion: Deceptively relaxed but ready to move in a swift blur without signaling any warning. If Doc and Raider hadn't known him to be a ranch hand, they'd have pegged him right off for a gunfighter.

He stopped when he was less than twenty feet away from them. He said nothing for a moment, directing his eyes toward Raider—eyes that seemed queerly oiled with venom. At last he spoke, biting off each word as it came. "Raider, I'm here to say you're the granddaddy of every stinkin'polecat that ever lived. You're a lowdown snake that wiggles behind everyone's back, and the unwiped ass of a slope-headed Digger Indian."

Although Doc was not looking at Raider, he sensed his

partner's stiffening. In a low voice he said, "Easy, Rade. Don't give him what he wants."

Dillard threw a glance at Doc. "This is between me and Raider. Reckon you better step aside, Weatherbee."

"Any quarrel you've got with Raider, you've got with me, too," said Doc.

"Doc," said Raider quickly, "I can handle this misguided sodbuster. Just give me the room I need."

Frowning, Doc moved away from what might turn out to be the line of fire. He would rather have done the talking, for he prided himself on being as handy with words as Raider was with a gun, but Raider's stubborn look now said he'd make love to a sheep before he'd allow Doc or anyone else to help him.

"Seems you don't mind bein' called names," Dillard said to Raider. "Or maybe you're just too scared shitless to do anything about it. Now, I wouldn't shoot no man in the back, but I'd admire it if you'd turn yours so's I could see the yellow streak in it."

"You're makin' a lot of talk, Dillard," Raider said calmly. "But it don't seem to say much. You mind tellin' me just why you've got a burr in your craw all of a sudden?"

"Why the hell do you think? You spent the night with Rina, you mangy saddlebum. Anybody who pushes himself on a fine lady like Rina Larkin has to answer to *me*!"

"So that's it. I'll be goddamned." Raider shook his head slightly. "You figure I'm poachin' on your territory."

"Enough talk, Raider. Let's see how fast you can draw."

"You first, Dillard," said Raider. "If you feel that lucky. I don't mind shootin' a varmint, but I hate like hell goin' to jail for it."

"Now, hold on both of you!" Doc called from the side. "Second man who draws is shooting in self-defense—that's the law. But it won't do him much good escaping a murder charge if he's lying there stone dead. And the first man to draw ain't any better off either way. The odds are, you both lose.''

"Stay out of it, Weatherbee," Dillard said, without taking his eyes from Raider.

"Doc's right," Raider said. "You want to unbuckle and settle this some other way, I'll be happy to oblige.''

"You feed on sheep manure!" said Dillard.

"That so?" said Raider mildly.

"Your ma was a clapped-up whore!" said Dillard, almost trembling in his agitation.

"I've heard better cussin' than that at a Sunday school picnic," Raider said.

"You're a lowdown, sidewindin', six-stitch sonofabitch!" said Dillard, his voice rising.

"That ain't cussin'," Raider said. "That's kind of a compliment.''

Dillard took a deep breath, as though to blow up a balloon, and his sun-scalded face turned purple with effort. He spouted out what must have been every cussword he knew plus a few he invented on the spot. "Raider, you are a pus-filled, desiccated, mummified mountain of weasel shit! The bastard son of an outhouse maggot! A long turd trailin' from a rattlesnake's ass! You're a warranteed, fourteen-carat, dyed-in-the-wool fucker of sheep and a poag-boy bungholed so often your farts sound like sighs! *When you gonna draw?*''

"When I see somethin' worth drawin' at," said Raider calmly.

The head of steam Dillard had been building up inside himself at last exploded. His eyes were wild as the last vestige of common sense he possessed blew away in the explosion. He went for his gun. His hand moved even faster than Doc had expected it might; it streaked to his holster and spirited the gun out of it all in one smooth motion Doc might have missed had he blinked while it happened.

A gunshot sounded in the torpid stillness of the street, so loud it stung Doc's eardrums.

It was Raider's gun that had spoken, not Dillard's.

Dillard, his face wide with surprise, flew backward as though hit by a swung railroad tie. He hit the ground hard, four feet from where he'd been standing, and his leg twitched several times, like that of a gut-slit frog, before he was absolutely still, his pale eyes glass marbles staring at the sky.

Doc stared at the dead man. "Jee-hosophat!" he said quietly.

Raider was stepping forward. The frown twisting his dark brows was one of puzzlement. He leaned over Dillard, peered at the hole in his chest and at the widening pool of blood beneath him, then straightened up and turned to Doc. "I couldn't have missed," he said.

"You didn't miss," said Doc. "Look at him."

"That's not what I mean." Raider seemed bewildered—it wasn't like him. "I shot for his legs, Doc. No use killin' the bastard so there'd be a big fuss about it. Now, I *could* have missed his damn leg—I ain't perfect—but not so much I'd get him in the heart instead."

"Well, it looks like you did just that," said Doc. "And as far as the big fuss is concerned, it looks like it's coming now."

Raider looked where Doc was nodding. Men were piling out of the Grand Palace saloon and rushing toward them. Along the street, other doors were opening, and white, surprised faces were appearing. Within moments, Raider, Doc, and the dead body sprawled in the dust were surrounded by a crowd of people.

Marshal Dan Carver stepped out of it. His gun was drawn, and his lean, pockmarked face was expressionless except for a slight nervous twitch at the corner of his mouth. He said, "Gonna drop that hogleg, Raider, or do I have to blast you like you did poor Dillard?"

Raider's frown deepened as he tossed his gun down.

"Fair fight, marshal," he said. "Don't get your bowels in an uproar."

"That's right," said Doc. "Dillard drew first."

"That's what *you* say, Weatherbee. Any other witnesses?" His eyes scanned the faces of the crowd. There were only blank stares. He turned to two of his deputies, who were standing behind him. "All right, boys," he said. "Get the cuffs on both of 'em."

"*Both* of them?" said Doc. "Goddamn it, I was just standing here!"

Carver looked at him evenly. "Murder and accessory to same," he said. "Both against the law—even here in Tamarack Springs."

The cell, which evidently hadn't been occupied a great deal lately, had a musty smell to it. A cockroach came out of the ticking that lay on the iron cot and ran down its leg to the stone floor. Raider reached out with his boot and squashed it.

"Rade," sighed Doc, "this time you really fucked things up."

"I've had enough o' your complaints!" roared Raider, springing to his feet. "Square off, you bastard!"

"Not that I wouldn't like to oblige you," said Doc, "but here and now's the wrong time and place. Now calm down and let's see if we can't think our way out of this."

"Think? Think, hell! We've got to *do* somethin'!"

"Right. After we figure exactly what kind of pickle we're in. Now, the way I look at it, my statement as a witness would have counted for something anyplace else. But the marshal *wants* us here in the pokey, so he's nabbed us both on a murder charge. The hell of it is, he might make it stick. A jury could find it hard to believe Dillard drew first. How come, they're gonna ask, he never got a chance to fire before you put a slug in his chest?"

"You pig-headed bastard, that's the point," said Raider. "I *didn't* put that slug in his chest!"

"Raider, if you shot at his leg and missed by that much, I'm surprised too. But he surer'n hell took one in the heart, and if you didn't put it there, who did?"

"Goddamned if I know! Somebody up the street, maybe. Somebody aimin' out of some goddamn window."

"Maybe," said Doc thoughtfully. "But if it sounds doubtful to me, think how everybody else is going to look at it. You were after Rina and all her money, they'll say. Dillard was in your way. So you picked a fight with him and blew him off the street. With me along to help you out. We, the jury, find the defendants guilty of murder and recommend they get their necks stretched. Next case."

Raider glowered. "Doc," he said, "they've got us by the balls."

"They sure have," said Doc. "And they haven't even started squeezing yet."

Doc and Raider spent the rest of the afternoon going over every inch of the cell in the wild hope of finding a way out of it. It lay on a corridor just off the marshal's office, and any preparations they might have made for an escape attempt wouldn't have been seen, but that wasn't of much help, because as far as they could tell there were no preparations that would do any good. The cell portion of the building was built of solid rock. The bars on the tiny, high window that overlooked a rear alley were thick and firm. They might have chinked away at the mortar between the rocks if they'd had something to chink with, but that, they estimated, would take days—weeks maybe—and it was doubtful they'd be here that long.

It was dark outside before they heard a step in the corridor and saw the glow of an approaching kerosene lantern. A moment later Dan Carver stood in front of the cell with the shadowed figures of his deputies—one of whom held the lantern—grouped behind him. Carver's pistol was drawn.

"Raider," he said, "we're goin' for a little stroll. Doc, you back up to the wall and stay there while Raider steps out. And no tricks. I'm fast with this iron, like maybe you heard.''

As Doc watched, puzzled, the marshal took Raider from the cell and disappeared with him. Raider, Doc noticed, was a wound-up spring, ready to make a break at the slightest opportunity. But Carver, even after Raider was handcuffed, kept his distance and continued to hold his gun as though not only willing but eager to use it.

The night air was cool outside. Raider was prodded around to the back of the jail building, and then toward the knoll at the edge of town where the whorehouse stood, the lights in its windows bright yellow patches in the darkness.

He looked at the marshal. ''Where we goin'? There?''

''Shut up and keep walkin', Raider,'' Carver said.

Raider, somewhat to his regret, had not yet had a chance for a close inspection of the whorehouse, and this time, as he neared it and saw all its bay and dormer windows and the crenellated decorations along its eaves, he realized that it must be the biggest and fanciest residential structure in town, rivaling some of the spacious houses found in wealthy city neighborhoods.

He was brought to the rear of the house. A slanted cellar door was open and he was steered into it. Here, he descended a long flight of steps until he came to a heavy oak double door. When Carver stepped past him and pounded on it, it opened.

Winfield Brent stood there, smiling coldly at Raider.

''Evenin', Mr. Raider,'' said Brent. ''It's about time you came callin' for that little talk we never got around to.''

Stepping inside, Raider found himself in a huge cellar room, which immediately struck him as more like a dungeon than the ordinary basement of a house. The walls were of mortared rock, and huge beams crossed the ceiling overhead, where there must have been plenty of thickness between this lower level and the house that rested upon it, for not a sound of the revelry above could be heard here.

Lanterns hung from the ceiling beams and illuminated the center of the room, where there was a table with several chairs around it. On the table was a whiskey bottle flanked by glasses. Brent turned, went to the table, and sat down. "Take off his cuffs, Dan," he said, nodding at Raider, "and leave him here with me."

Carver looked surprised. "Alone?"

"We won't be alone." Brent's smile was poised and confident. He glanced toward the darkened corner of the room. "Come on over here, Turk."

Raider had his second look at Turk, whom he remembered from the day Brent had first approached him in the Grand Palace. In this low-ceilinged, dungeonlike cellar room he looked as big as a grizzly reared up on its hind legs. Naked from the waist up, Turk was a mound of fat-slabbed muscle. His hairless head glistened in the light of the hanging lanterns; his mustaches swept out on each side like a pair of Texas longhorns. He glowered at Raider as though sizing him up.

After Carver had removed Raider's handcuffs and stepped out of the room, shutting the heavy door, Brent nodded at the chair across from him. "Sit down, Mr. Raider. Make yourself comfortable. For the time bein'."

Brent poured a drink and slid it toward Raider. Raider, still saying nothing, and with his eyes moving about warily, took the chair he'd been offered and settled his eyes on Brent. He knew very well that Brent's easy manner—that of a plantation owner entertaining an honored guest—was meant to keep him off guard, but, even knowing it, he found it difficult to avoid relaxing. He tossed down some of the drink. Good whiskey—better than the rotgut at the bar of the Grand Palace.

"All right, Brent," he said finally. "It's your play."

Brent leaned back, smiled, and sipped his own whiskey. "I'd introduce you to Turk, here," he said, "but he doesn't understand much English and hasn't much use for civilities. Interesting fellow, Turk. He was gelded as a prisoner of war back in his own part of the world, and that makes him eminently suitable for his present duties as a bouncer and general handyman in the establishment above us, where, because of his unfortunate condition, he is unable to sample the merchandise.''

"Come on, Brent," Raider interrupted. "That ain't what you brought me here to tell me."

"On the contrary," said Brent smoothly. "It's an important part of our little discussion. You see, Turk appreciates the protection I give him from several murder charges hangin' over him elsewhere. He didn't mean to break all those necks. It's just that he doesn't know his own strength. It wouldn't be wise for you to attempt to leave here forcibly before we've had a chance to talk, Mr. Raider, would it?''

Raider looked up at Turk. Turk smiled down at him. Raider sighed. He was forced to agree with what Brent had just said.

"The other thing about Turk," Brent continued, "is that he's quite adept at inflictin' torture. He knows ways the Apache Indians haven't dreamed of yet. And that is why, Mr. Raider, you will do well to answer all my questions truthfully.''

"What questions?" asked Raider.

"I think you know what questions. But I'm a fair and reasonable man, Mr. Raider. So I'll ask them nice and politely first. If that doesn't work''—he sipped his drink again—"I will be forced to call on Turk for his assistance.''

CHAPTER FOURTEEN

The rest of the whiskey warmed Raider's throat as it went down. He was keeping himself as relaxed as Winfield Brent; in effect, playing the same game: Relaxed on the surface, but taut and alert within, measuring his chances. At the moment they didn't seem too favorable. He'd noticed that Brent wasn't packing a gun, but that in itself, he knew, was a precaution; with no gun on hand, Raider wouldn't be able to get it for himself, should he move fast and get lucky. As for a sudden attack, Brent would be no problem, but Turk would. Looking at the eunuch's looming hulk and fat-encased muscles, Raider decided that this was one man he probably wouldn't be able to take, not even with the dirtiest fighting tricks he knew.

"All right, Brent," Raider said finally. "You're figurin' on makin' me talk. Though I'm damned if I know what about. You set the whole thing up—the gunfight with Dillard—"

Brent smiled and nodded. "Dillard came into town, lookin' for you, shootin' his mouth off about it. I knew you'd outdraw him, but I couldn't be sure you'd kill him. It was no problem to station a man with a rifle and make sure it turned out the way it did."

"Seems to me you went to a lot of trouble," drawled Raider. "You mind tellin' me why?"

"Still playin' dumb? All right, I'll go along with it—for just a minute or two. You and that partner of yours blow into town pretendin' to be vets. A blind Siwash Indian can see you're not. Lawmen? I don't think so—extradition doesn't hold here in the Springs, and lawmen know it. Bounty hunters? They can't take anybody here either; we make sure of that. Which leaves one thing. You and Doc are on the same side of the law as everybody else who drifts this way. But you didn't come to hole up, like our other visitors. You came here lookin' for somethin', didn't you?"

"Lookin' for what?"

"Ever hear of a man named William Flood?"

"Can't say as I have."

"I believe you're lyin', Raider. I think you know that William Flood got out of prison more than a year ago and that he's bound to show up here—maybe any day now. He, or somebody actin' on his behalf. Somebody slick, just like you and Doc Weatherbee."

Raider shook his head. "I still don't know what you're talkin' about."

"I have the feelin'," said Brent, "that you not only know what I'm talkin' about, but what I'm after and where it is. And I might add that I've been waitin' years for it and have no intention of lettin' it slip out of my fingers now."

"Sorry. None o' this makes sense to me."

"I expected you might be stubborn, Mr. Raider," said Brent, glancing up at Turk and then down at Raider again. "Let's review the situation. You can't get what you came for now—you're on your way to hangin' for murder. But Dan Carver dances to whatever tune I play, and I can get those charges dropped. I'll do better than that, Mr. Raider. I'll see that you and your partner ride out of here with a fair share. Let's say ten percent. Even that's enough to put you in clover the rest of your lives. All you have to do is tell me exactly where it's tucked away."

"Brent," said Raider, "what if—just what if—you're *really* barkin' up the wrong tree? What if I don't know a damn thing to tell you, even if I wanted to?"

"In that case," Brent said suavely, "I haven't lost a thing, though I'm afraid you have. First you, then your partner. Turk here will bring you to the point where most men will talk. If you haven't by then, I'll know for sure you're of no use to me. When something's of no use to me, I get rid of it. Shot while tryin' to escape—that ought to do it."

Raider wasn't given to working things out step by step in his mind, the way Doc was. That was usually too slow for him. But when cornered, he did come to lightning-quick decisions, translating them into action immediately— the risks somehow weighed without a great deal of careful thought. It was like that now. A wild-animal sense told him that this wasn't perhaps an ideal moment for making a play, but it also told him that it was the best that would come along. Brent, smugly pleased with himself, was leaning back, as relaxed as he ever would be. Turk, not understanding much of what was being said, had drifted off into a vague state of boredom.

Raider shot up from his chair, knocking it aside. In the same blurring motion he propelled himself at angle toward the looming eunuch who towered over him, slamming the top of his head into the man's chin with the force of a cannonball.

Turk did not budge. The pain of the blow went all the way down into the pulp of Raider's teeth and sparks started to fly in swirls in front of his eyes.

He saw Turk's monstrous arms rise, with his hands clasped together. Still trying to regain his balance, he saw them come down again. They smashed into the back of his neck, knocking him all the way to the floor. He shook his head to get rid of the block of calf's-foot jelly in which it now seemed to be encased, but the thick daze wouldn't leave him.

Turk reached down and picked him up. Turk encircled his torso with his arms, just below the rib cage, and began to squeeze. Raider felt the breath whoosh out of him. Blackness descended over his eyes, the flashing sparks stayed for another moment, and then, suddenly, he wasn't feeling anything.

Doc, in his cell, was wishing more than ever that he possessed Raider's ability to doze off at will when there wasn't anything else to do, because that would have passed the time one hell of a lot better than the restless pacing he'd been engaged in.

With luck, he was thinking, he might dream. With even greater luck the dream might be about Heather or Virtue or any of another hundred girls he'd known or, with greatest luck, some gal he'd never known. Those were the ones you really remembered—those you didn't make it with.

Several times he'd gone to the small, high window, tiptoed up to look out of it, and searched the moonlit semidarkness outside for some sign of Raider returning. As far as Doc had been able to make out, Carver and his deputies had walked Raider in the direction of the whorehouse on its little knoll at the edge of town, and he was still wondering why in hell they'd gone that way. Maybe, he thought wildly, they were treating him to a last roll in the hay—the way a condemned man is served a fancy meal before he dies.

That was how your thoughts went when you had nothing to do but think; they danced around in your head like the unreal spirits you thought you saw after chewing on a peyote button.

He wasn't sure how much time had passed since they'd taken Raider away. His railroad watch, along with his gun and all his other possessions, was stashed somewhere in the marshal's office, and, from the sound of things, that had been empty all along. That in itself was a sign, like the stillness of a hillside when hostile Indians lurk upon it.

Something out of the ordinary was going on. Something ominous.

Suddenly he heard the sound of the front door opening—not loudly, but as though someone was opening it in stealth. He stepped away from the cell door and put his back flat to the wall as footsteps came down the cell corridor.

A moment later there was a shadowed figure just outside the bars. Doc remained motionless, hoping that would also make him invisible for the time being.

"Doc?" It was Heather Ormsby's voice in the darkness.

"Oh. It's you." He stepped away from the wall.

She was at the door; there was a clinking of metal, and it swung open. He could see her boyish figure and tousled blond hair more clearly now. "Spare keys in the town office," she explained. "But I had to wait till things got quiet. Why in hell did you and Raider have to shoot that bastard and get yourselves thrown in here?"

"We didn't shoot him. Tell you about that later. Let's get out of here before somebody comes back."

"Lucky nobody's here. Didn't expect that. I was wondering how I'd be able to sneak past whoever was on guard."

They were both striding down the corridor now and into the marshal's office, where a kerosene lamp burned with the wick turned down low. "They've got Raider," said Doc. "I don't know what for, though I can guess. Private questioning. Last I saw they were headed toward the whorehouse."

"The whorehouse?" Heather's eyebrows rose. "Then it *is* questioning. It was built on the foundation of an old fort. You can't hear a thing that goes on in the cellar. Brent and his crowd have used it before to make somebody talk."

Doc was searching the drawers of the marshal's desk, and a moment later he found his and Raider's gunbelts, plus his railroad watch, which he returned to his vest pocket. He strapped both gunbelts around his middle, with his own Diamondback on the right and Raider's .44 on the left. His eye lighted upon his curl-brim derby, which hung on a peg on the wall. He retrieved that, too, and donned it at a cocky angle.

"Never mind making yourself pretty," said Heather, in that tomboyish voice of hers. "You've got to get your ass out of town lickety-split. You'll have to bust into the livery stable to get horses. I can wiggle through the back window."

"You're a good gal, Heather," said Doc, "and maybe someday I can thank you proper. But you go on back home now. I'm gonna see what I can do to spring Raider loose."

"I'm going with you," she said.

"Like hell you are," said Doc.

"Like hell I'm not," she answered. "Come on."

In his time, Raider had known cuts, bruises, broken bones, scalds and burns, bullet wounds, and once, from a pair of new boots, the granddaddy of all bunions. The pain from these hadn't even come close to the pain he was experiencing now.

Turk and Winfield Brent had him flat upon the rock wall. Iron spikes with rings had been driven into it, and his wrists and ankles were lashed to these, so that he was spread out in the form of a standing X. He was also naked. The blows to his midsection Turk had delivered, apparently for pleasure, had been bad enough, even with Raider bracing his stomach muscles to receive them. But Turk had now affixed a loop of waxed fishing line to his testicles and was standing in front of it, holding its end, and grinning under his longhorn mustaches. Whenever Brent nodded, Turk would pull the line hard, tightening the loop, making it cut into his balls and squeeze them with excruciating pain.

"I can keep this up till dawn, Mr. Raider," said Brent.

"But I don't believe you can. All right, once more. Where are all those gold coins hidden?"

Murmuring in a hoarse voice through the pain, which persisted after each tightening of the loop, spreading up through all his groin, Raider said, "Don't . . . know."

Brent nodded.

Turk tightened the loop again.

A wave of grayness started to wash up over Raider's vision. He'd felt that coming with increasing force along with each stab of pain when the loop was tightened. Now, suddenly, he thought he knew a way to gain at least a brief respite from the agony.

"Where is it, Raider? *Where is it?*"

"Don't . . . know."

The hard purse string cut into the sack, crushing the nuggets within it. Each time before he had grimaced involuntarily, and, while he'd managed to keep from screaming, he'd been unable to contain a series of choking gasps. This time he called upon all his willpower—remaining drops of it he wasn't even sure he possessed—to hold back both the grimace and his grunting cry. Instead, he closed his eyes, letting his head fall to one side, and his entire body become limp.

"Sonofabitch," he heard Brent say. "Not as tough as I thought he was. All right, Turk, untie him, and we'll see if we can bring him to. Then we'll start all over again."

Outside the cellar door, Marshal Carver slouched against the wall of the building, rolling himself a cigarette. He poured the dry tobacco flakes from their cotton sack into the paper curved in his hand, closed the string with his teeth, tucked the sack away, ran his tongue over the edge of the paper, then rolled it deftly with one hand.

It was quiet now. The lights in the whorehouse windows had been doused, and there was no more sound of laughter and piano music from within. Whatever sounds the gals and their customers were making now—groans and mur-

murs and little squeals, Dan Carver didn't doubt—were no longer audible through the solid walls of the well-built mansion. As for the cellar, well, all the banshees of Hell could be howling in there and a body would never know.

Just wait, Brent had told him. He'd known it would be a long time—that hombre who called himself Raider wouldn't crack easily. He'd sent his deputies away, finding their company not particularly entertaining, and much preferring his own.

There were times when Dan Carver was tempted to leave Tamarack Springs and go somewhere to hire out his gun again, not as a lawman for a lawman's measly pay, but as a professional killer who would either scare men off or gun them down, according to the wishes of the clients that could always be found. But that was a lonely life that kept a man walking on tiptoe and looking warily at shadows all the time, and now he was no longer young, and he was a little tired of it. Brent paid him well, over and above his salary as town marshal, and his job as a peace officer was ordinarily easy, what with all the outlaws who blew into town agreeing to behave themselves as long as they stayed. Truth was, Tamarack Springs had less crime, on the whole, than any so-called respectable town, unless you counted Dodge City and Abilene in their heyday.

He thumbnailed a match and lit his cigarette. The glow of the match illuminated his sharp profile, which resembled a hatchet with nicks and chips in the blade.

A figure appeared at the far corner of the house. Without even bothering to stare at it more closely, Carver drew his gun in a swift motion and spat the cigarette from his mouth.

"Why, Dan, you crazy cuss," said the figure in a breathy female voice he recognized immediately, "don't point that goddamn hogleg at *me*."

"Heather," he said, "what the hell are *you* doin' here?"

She was coming toward him. In the moonlight he could make out her pale, tousled hair and the slim fit of her jeans around that taut, boyish rump of hers. Once, in prison, Dan Carver had had himself a boy or two, but that had been an emergency measure, and he'd never really preferred the practice. Gals had been made for it, and gals were better, all things considered. Especially gals like this wild little heifer coming toward him now. He'd heard she didn't mind putting out for some of the boys around town, and he'd had his eye on her, in a passing way, for some time.

"I've been looking for you, Dan. Couldn't sleep . . . slipped out of the house."

She was nearer now, and he saw that she was smiling. It didn't occur to him that this was an odd story she was telling; he didn't bother to ask himself how she'd known he'd be here behind the whorehouse. All he could think of was that suddenly something he'd wanted all along was being handed to him on a silver platter. He tucked his gun back into its holster. He grinned, and he meant it to be a pleasant grin, but, spread across that hatchet face of his, it wasn't. "Lookin' for *me*, huh?" he said.

"Damn right." She was all the way up to him now; he could sense the warmth of her young, solid body. "I've been watching you, Dan, and you've been watching me. Those boys I've been fooling around with aren't half the man you are."

"That so?" Carver was staring at her in surprise, finding it hard to believe his luck.

Heather reached for the top buttons of her gingham shirt, opened them, and spread the shirt apart. Carver's eyes frogged out at what he saw. Her hard little breasts, with their peach-pink nipples, were staring out at him. Spittle formed at the edge of his mouth. He forgot everything else in the world—the quiet night around him, the lazy moon, the shadows, the sound of the breeze in the brush of the fields, everything but those inviting little mounds. On another occasion he might have heard the soft, scuffling step behind him. He did not hear it, and he reached out to touch those pouting little breasts.

Doc Weatherbee's gun slammed with cracking force into the back of his head, and the next thing he knew was blackness.

Heather looked down at Carver's body, slumped on the ground, and hurriedly rebuttoned her shirt. Doc stepped forward and came up beside her. "In there, " said Heather, nodding at the cellar door in its slanted box.

They descended the steps and, in the lantern-lighted vestibule, saw the heavy oak doors. Iron hasps to hold a bar protruded from them, but the bar had been set aside and was leaning against the wall. Cautiously, Doc pulled at one door, opening it enough to make a crack he could peer through. He saw the big room inside, and he saw Winfield Brent standing near one wall with a huge, bald, mustachioed man, stripped to the waist, beside him. Both were staring down at Raider, who was birthday naked and sprawled on the floor.

Almost immediately both men detected his presence and whirled toward him, startled. His Diamondback drawn, Doc stepped inside.

"Evening, gents," said Doc. "Looks like a private party, but I think I'll join it anyway."

The big man, his eyes wild, came charging toward Doc.

"Turk!" Brent snapped at him.

He didn't hear, or, if he did, he didn't care; he kept coming.

"Don't try it!" cautioned Doc.

He didn't seem to hear that, either. He was almost upon Doc, arms spread for a bear hug, when Doc reluctantly pulled the trigger of the stub-barreled .38. The sound of the explosion numbed Doc's ears as it slammed in instantaneous echo back and forth between the rock walls. It would have thrown a normal man back, but Turk, with an ugly hole in his midriff where the slug had entered, kept coming. He crashed into Doc and bore him down to the floor.

Everything after that happened so swiftly that Doc could scarcely keep track of it. As he lay there, pinned, Heather reached down and slipped the .44 out of the holster on his left side. She put the muzzle to the side of Turk's head, cocked the hammer, and pulled the trigger, blasting most of his shiny skull away.

In the same instant, Brent, seeing her occupied, whirled and sprang toward her. Raider, on the floor where he'd been playing possum, reached out, grabbed Brent's ankle, tripped him, and sent him sprawling facedown.

Doc finally wriggled out from under Turk's deadweight and rose to his feet, trying not to let Raider see how shaky he felt. It wasn't pretty, the way Turk's blood and bits of bone and brain were strewn all over the floor. Raider rose, glowered down at Brent, said, "Stay there, you bastard," then crossed the room to retrieve his clothes.

Heather watched him. Her eyes glowed a little. Doc could guess what part of Raider they were focused on. He took the .44 out of her hand gently, scooped up his own Diamondback, and used both weapons to keep Brent in place while Heather kept her admiring gaze on Raider's whipcord thighs and the huge appendage that hung between them.

CHAPTER FIFTEEN

The dawn, somewhere on the other side of the mountains, was putting a layer of iridescent mother-of-pearl across the sky. Doc and Raider pushed their horses forward at a light jog toward the foothills.

"Doc," said Raider, "I hope you're right about makin' tracks in this direction."

"Of course I'm right," Doc said firmly. "It'll be a while before anybody lets Brent and the marshal out of that cellar, but once they're loose they'll round up some men and start looking for us. They'll figure we've headed for Yancy to get on the train. If we had gone there, they might catch up with us before the train came through. So instead we'll hole up at Uriah Van Hawley's cabin."

"And then what?" asked Raider.

"I don't know," said Doc. "One step at a time."

Before long they had reached the slope where Uriah's cabin lay nestled in the trees. They were deliberately noisy in their approach, figuring that was the best way to let Uriah know they were coming. He was waiting for them in the clearing when they arrived. He had a rifle leveled, and Tumbleweed, with her big, half-scared eyes, was standing behind him with a shotgun. Uriah lowered his rifle as they halted their horses, contemplated them for a moment, and pulled on his long, knitted beard. "So it's you two," he said.

"Our apologies for the early call," said Doc, dismounting. "And since it is so early, how about some breakfast?"

"You sure don't mind inviting yourself, do you?" said Uriah. "All right. Come on in."

By the time Tumbleweed had coffee and cornmeal mush on the table, they had told Uriah most of what had happened and explained why they had ridden out here to his cabin.

Uriah, whose facial expression was hard to see through all the tangled hair that covered it, seemed to be thoughtful. "So you two are after William Flood's hidden loot too, eh? I'm not surprised. Everybody who hears about it is. I've been hoping to find it myself. Only I'm not sure how I'd ever be able to sneak off with it if I did. I'm no gunfighter, and I'd have one hell of a time holding on to it. But if I had a couple of partners, like you gents—"

"Stop right there," said Doc. He looked at Raider. "Shall we tell him who we really are?"

Raider nodded. "I reckon we can chance it," he said.

Doc turned to Uriah again. "We're Pinkerton operatives, Uriah. We came here on another matter and ran into this treasure thing. It wouldn't be ours, even if we did find it. But with that much money, the rewards themselves amount to a small fortune. If your information makes finding it possible, you'd share in those rewards. Since you can't seem to handle the whole cake all by yourself, you'd be better off, and a lot safer, settling for just a slice of it. All you have to do is tell us everything you know—and I've got an idea that's considerable."

Uriah was silent for a long moment before he finally said, "All right. It all begins with Millie."

"With who?" asked Doc.

"Sweetest little gal you ever saw," said Uriah, "even if she did hire herself out to anybody who had the price. What the hell; she had to make a living too."

Raider and Doc traded puzzled glances.

"When I first came here," Uriah continued, "and be-

fore Tumbleweed showed up, I used to visit the whorehouse occasionally. I might explain I've got something of
a problem in that respect, but Millie was always very
patient with me, and with her I was able to enjoy at least a
measure of satisfaction. She cottoned to me, too. Maybe
because I wasn't as rough with her as her other customers.
In fact, she started to get ideas that maybe I could take her
away, and we'd get hitched up, and then, like they say,
live happily ever afterward.''

"What's all this got to do with anything?" asked Raider.

"I'm getting to it," said Uriah, in a tone of mild
rebuke. "It seems this William Flood also got sweet on
Millie when he was here. Nobody knew he was Flood
when he blew in; he'd changed his name and pretended he
was an outlaw who had just made off with a wagonload of
arms and ammunition from an Army depot. Nobody dreamed
it wasn't weapons he had in all those heavy boxes, and
Brent made him welcome for the usual price, the same as
he did anybody on the owl hoot. Flood was a clever man
and somehow managed to hide his loot under all their
noses, which was his plan from the beginning. He was
willing to wait years, if necessary, until his robbery was
half forgotten, before he retrieved his spoils and started to
enjoy them without bringing a passel of government agents
or bounty hunters down on his neck. As you know, Flood
went off to San Francisco, got recognized there and thrown
in prison. I'm sure the authorities tried their damnedest to
make him tell what he'd done with all that gold, but he
never did talk.''

"Are you saying he told this gal, Millie, what he was
really up to? Is that it?" asked Doc.

"Not exactly," said Uriah. "But he did get a little too
drunk now and then and mumble a few hints to Millie. I
guess his one weakness was a need to brag to somebody
about how clever he'd been. Millie didn't realize what
he'd been talking about until later, after he'd gone. By that
time the San Francisco newspapers, with word of Flood's

arrest, had reached Tamarack Springs, and she put two and two together. This had to be the same man who'd been telling her how rich he was going to be. Millie never told a soul about it, except me. She wanted me to help her find that treasure, so we could both go off with it.''

Uriah sipped his hot coffee, sighed, and stared off into the air for a moment.

"How come you and this Millie ain't still lookin' for it?'' asked Raider.

"Poor Millie," said Uriah. "She was crossing the street in town one day when this runaway team of horses came along. The wagon wheels went right over her, and I guess she died quickly, without too much pain.''

"Quite a story," said Doc. "But if Millie was the only one Flood talked to, how did Brent get wind of the treasure?''

"You have to remember," Uriah explained, "that Winfield Brent pays close attention to newcomers. After all the news came in, he remembered the man with all those ammunition boxes, when everybody else had more or less forgotten him. He put two and two together, same as Millie did. I've no doubt he checked further, sending for pictures and that sort of thing. Brent knew he didn't have a chance of finding the loot just digging around for it, with no idea of where to dig. The thing to do was wait till Flood got out of prison, then let Flood lead him to it. That would take years, but it was worth it. He's been sitting here, conducting business as usual, all this time, just waiting for Flood to show up.''

"Or somebody Flood might have sent in his stead," said Doc, nodding. "Which explains how he got so suspicious of me and Raider.''

"You showed up at an unfortunate time," said Uriah. "Flood just got out of prison, maybe close to a year ago. Chances are he's been busy backtracking, shaking off whatever lawmen they must have sent to follow him. As soon as he feels he's free and clear, he'll be here. Which could be any day now.''

"This whole thing," mused Raider, "has got more tangles to it than a ball of yarn the cat got hold of.''

"Right," said Doc. "But if we could spot Flood when he came in, we could watch him too, and recover the loot ourselves. Do you know what he looks like, Uriah?''

Uriah shook his head "Millie never described him. I expect Brent's got his picture somewhere—maybe in those 'wanted' posters the marshal collects—but I wouldn't know him from Adam's off-ox. And suppose you could recognize him? You can't go back into town now, with a murder charge hanging over you. It's my guess Carver will add this eunuch's murder to it; he won't want to tip his hand by going after Ormsby's daughter, and Carver's not going to admit she made a fool of him the way she did. All he can do now is find you two and make damn sure he doesn't bring you back alive.''

"Well, I'll tell you," said Doc, leaning back from his meal and patting his pearl-gray vest in satisfaction. "We've got some thinking to do before we make the next move. I suggest we get down to Yancy as soon as the coast is clear and telegraph the home office for a description of William Flood. After that we can figure some way to get back into town.''

"There's no telegraph office in Yancy," Uriah said.

"I've got a key and a battery," Doc explained. "In our saddlebags. I made sure I fetched 'em from the wagon before we hightailed it out here. Anyway, we'll just relax ourselves for the time being. That'll give us a chance to think it out a little better.''

Uriah rose from his chair. The way his whiskers spread seemed to indicate that there was a broad smile under them. "As long as you're here, Doc, we can finally get around to that chess game.''

"Capital idea," said Doc, also rising.

"Chess," said Raider sourly. "Slowest game I ever did see."

Tumbleweed, reading Raider's lips, brightened and held up a checker piece for Raider to see.

"No, I ain't gonna play checkers, either," Raider said. "You got a deck o' cards, Uriah? I'll see if I can bust it, for a change, with solitaire."

CHAPTER SIXTEEN

Raider looked down at Doc from his perch atop the telegraph pole, where he held himself in place by hooking one arm over the crossbar. "This is the last time I do your monkey-climbin' for you, Doc. Absolutely the last time, you hear?"

"What are you complaining about?" Doc called up to him. "We flipped a coin, and you lost. What could be fairer than that?"

"Next time we'll use *my* coin," grumbled Raider.

"Come on, Rade," said Doc wearily. "We're wasting time. Hook into the line."

The wire Raider had carried aloft terminated in a specially made spring clip and, from this, led down to Doc, below, who had already laid out his paraphernalia on the ground—a seven-pound battery jar containing blue vitriol as the electrolyte for zinc and copper anodes, and a standard nickel-plated Western Union lever key. Of the many poles along the railroad line, they had chosen this one for a particular reason. It was almost a half mile east of the hamlet of Yancy and below a slight rise, so that Doc, Raider, and their horses couldn't be seen from the town, while Raider, once he reached the top of the pole, had a clear view of its dusty main street, the water tower, and the several scattered structures that gave it the excuse for being called a town.

"Quiet as a dead man's eyes," he'd called down, after his first quick observation.

Several days had passed since they'd arrived at Uriah Van Hawley's cabin. Doc had spent them in a series of long-drawn-out chess games with the bearded ex-teacher, losing most of them but achieving at least four wins and two draws. Raider had fidgeted, gone for long walks in the woods by himself, and killed some time adding to his knowledge of Indian sign language under Tumbleweed's tutelage.

During their stay at the cabin, Uriah had sortied into Tamarack Springs, returning to report that Marshal Dan Carver and a posse, looking for Doc and Raider, had already been to Yancy and returned. The whole town was buzzing with the story that bent the truth some and made the marshal look heroic instead of foolish. And Doc and Raider were now charged with the murder of one Safavid Khalifa, otherwise known as Turk. Heather Ormsby, who knew the real story, was keeping quiet about it; anything she said would be her word against Carver's and Brent's, so, quite sensibly, she was saying nothing.

Doc now squatted down beside his gear and began to click the key with the skillful wrist motion he'd acquired. He'd been offered jobs on occasion as a telegraph operator, but, not caring to be confined to an office, he'd turned them down.

Long minutes passed. Doc knew that along the line other operators were picking up his coded address and, according to their instructions, relaying it all the way to Chicago, patching in what soon would be a direct line between himself and the operator on duty in the Pinkerton office. Wagner, old Allan Pinkerton's chief assistant for field operations, would then be standing over the operator, getting the messages from him verbally as they came in, and dictating his responses.

Raider, atop the pole, cussed and grumbled as Doc's key remained silent, and as the hot sun crossed a visible arc overhead. Doc killed the time by smoking a Virgina cheroot, which, since it gave Doc comfort and pleasure, irritated Raider all the more.

At last Doc's key began to click with an incoming message. With a stub of a pencil he jotted notes in the small school lesson book that was part of his telegraph equipment. This procedure was also long drawn out, and Raider continued to cuss impatiently, with Doc waving for him to be quiet each time.

A good hour went by before Raider was able to slide down from the pole and stomp on the ground to drive away the pins and needles in his leg joints. He glared while Doc studied his notes and finally blurted out, "Well, goddamn it, what did Wagner say?"

"Too much, as usual," said Doc. "But what it boils down to is this. We're assigned to track down the stolen coins, if we can—the agency got the case years ago and it's still on the books. We're also supposed to come up with some kind of proof that the fires were arson, so the insurance company won't have to pay off."

"They don't want much, do they?" growled Raider. "Did you tell 'em we're wanted for murder?"

"That's a detail I figured was beside the point," Doc said blandly. "But meanwhile we've got a description of this hombre, William Flood, just in case he shows up. Five foot nine, hundred and eighty pounds, stocky build, red hair, scar on the left side of his face, which he got from a knife fight in prison. I don't recall seeing anyone like that up in the Springs, though the general description could fit lots of men, and I guess a beard might hide that scar. So if he's there, it could be damn near anybody."

"Looks to me like we're right back where we started," grumbled Raider.

Doc was thoughtful. "If Flood's in these parts, he probably came through Yancy on the train. He *could* be around, you know, holed up, waiting for a chance to get the loot and slip out again. That gold must be mighty

heavy, and it wouldn't be easy to walk out with it unob-
served; it might take as much clever planning as getting it
there in the first place. Why don't we ride into Yancy and
see if anybody resembling Flood's been through there
lately?''

"You crazy, Doc? Them hotel people'd see us. They
must know by now we're wanted.''

"I wasn't thinking about the hotel.

"That skinny gal in the restaurant, huh? Goddamn it,
Doc, this is no time to go runnin' after a piece of ass.''

"Didn't have that in mind.''

"Bullshit. You ain't got a wakin' minute when it ain't
on your mind. But, well, maybe the skinny gal *did* see
somebody. And if you was as good to her as you say, she
wouldn't be inclined to turn us in. We hope, anyway.
Okay, Doc, let's take a chance. Except it's gotta be all
business. The longer we stay in Yancy, the more chance
we have of bein' spotted.''

Virtue Morgan looked up in surprise as they entered the
restaurant. They'd approached it by riding almost full
circle around the hamlet, taking partial cover in the rolling
land and entering the main street on the other side. They
hadn't seen a soul outside the hotel or any of the other
buildings; Yancy, as far as they could tell, was still in its
perpetual coma.

The brightly colored Mexican decorations, including the
serapes and Jalisco sombreros, were still on the walls of
the little establishment, and Virtue was in the same place
behind the counter, writing in her poetry book. She stared
at them for a moment. "Well, here you are—back again.
Knew you'd be and wondered when. I hear you got yourselves in trouble—''

"We sure did; the kind that's double," said Doc, finishing the rhyme for her. "Virtue, we're in a hurry—no time
to make poems. We got some important questions. Before
we ask them I want you to take my word for it that we

didn't murder anybody, if that's what you heard, and that we're actually on the side of the law.''

Virtue removed her Ben Franklin spectacles and looked thoughtful. "I won't turn you in, if that's what you're worried about. But I think you both better get out of here soon as you can. Joe's home. He wouldn't like you hanging around. You or anybody else."

"Who the hell's Joe?" asked Raider.

"Her husband," Doc explained. "He works for the railroad and hardly ever gets here. He and Virtue aren't exactly lovey-dovey. Or so she said. Is it still like that, Virtue?"

"No change," she admitted cautiously. "I don't suppose you decided to take me out of here, did you, Doc? I'll go with you, if you say."

Doc shook his head. "I don't want to lie to you, Virtue. I'm still not ready to hitch up permanent, not even with somebody I like as much as you." He looked around the room. "Where is Joe, anyway?"

"In the back room. Resting."

"Okay, then maybe you can answer our questions real quick. No time to explain all the ins and outs, but we're looking for a man named William Flood who maybe came through here recently on his way to Tamarack Springs. I know you watch the trains come in, and I thought maybe you might have seen this hombre. I doubt if he'd be using his real name. Anyway, he's red haired, five foot nine, stocky build, and has a scar on his left cheek."

Virtue's eyes widened and she stared back at them for a long, silent moment.

As the moment fell away, it suddenly came to Doc what had caused her curious reaction. It was like a burst of light in his mind; suddenly things began to fall into place. Abruptly, he widened his own eyes, then said, "Hell, yes! That picture on your wall!"

"That's right," said Virtue quietly.

"What picture on what wall, damn it?" asked Raider.

"That husband of hers who's hardly ever here," answered Doc. "The picture don't show his hair color, and that there scar of his is kind of in shadow—that's why I didn't tumble to it right away. Joe Morgan. Dollars to doughnuts, *he's* William Flood."

"If he is," asked Virtue, "what of it? He's not the only man out west who changed his name. Or did it on account of some trouble they got into."

Doc nodded. "True enough. And we're not here to turn Joe—or William, if that's who he is—over to the law. All we want to do is talk to him and maybe give him some good advice. Like, how he can stop being a hunted man and know a little peace and quiet for a change. You'll learn what it's all about later, but for now there's no time to explain it. We're going into the back room, Virtue, to pay a call on this husband of yours."

Virtue reached under the counter and then, to their absolute surprise, brought her hand up with a Colt .45 frontier revolver in it. "I'm afraid I can't let you do that, gentlemen," she said.

Doc stared. "What the hell!"

"Joe said nobody was to see him. I don't know what it's all about, and there's not much between me and Joe, but I'm not going to see him get into any more trouble than he already is."

"Trouble? What trouble?"

"Just get out of here," Virtue said. "The both of you. Real quiet and real fast. And don't come back again."

Her eyes were fastened on Doc, and this was not lost on Raider. He moved fast, throwing himself on the counter, crashing into Virtue and wrenching the gun from her hand as though all in one motion. He tossed the gun to Doc, who caught it, then untangled himself.

Virtue suddenly began to sob.

"No call for that," Doc said gently. "This is the best thing for everybody, including Joe. You'll see."

"Keep her outa the way, Doc," said Raider. "If Mr.

Flood's in that back room, he might not like us bargin' in on him.'' He drew his own gun.

Virtue shook her head quickly. "Joe won't be stopping you.''

"How do you know?'' asked Raider.

"Go on in there,'' she sighed. "Just don't hurt him any more than he is. Please.''

Virtue's meaning became clear the moment Raider carefully pushed open the door to the back room. Joe Morgan—or William Flood, if that was who he was—lay flat on his back on the bed, his eyes closed. The scar at the corner of his mouth was clearly visible. He was clad in a flannel union suit, its top buttons open to reveal most of his chest. Just below his chest was a bandage, wrapped around his torso. Most of it was blood-soaked.

Doc stepped to the bed quickly, bent over the man, and took his pulse. "Alive,'' he said. "Just barely.''

"He came here like that,'' Virtue said from behind Raider. "Staggering—I thought he was drunk. I guess that's what anyone who saw him thought. But it was the bullet that's still in him. No doctor, he said. I don't know why. I've been trying to make up my mind whether to get a doctor, anyway.''

Doc hunkered down a little farther and brought his lips close to the man's ear. "Can you hear me, Flood? Come on, wake up if you can.''

The man's eyes fluttered open. He saw Doc, rolled them in panic, and tried to pull away. The effort was too much for him and he fell back again. He began to breathe heavily, his face contorted in pain. "All right . . . I give up,'' he said, his voice hoarse and barely audible. "Tired of running . . . too damn tired . . .''

"Take it easy, Flood,'' said Doc. "We're not the law, and we're not after your loot—not for ourselves, anyway. We're Pinkerton men. What happened to you, anyway?''

"Got spotted in Provo, Utah . . . another one o' them bastards after my gold . . . I left him dead. . . .''

"But he left you this way, huh? And with everybody and his cousin looking for you, you couldn't risk getting yourself doctored."

Flood nodded weakly. "Thought I'd thrown most of 'em off the trail. Been workin' for the railroad . . . always movin' around. Set myself up here in Yancy, where I could wait . . . near to where the gold is. . . ."

"You don't have to explain it all," Doc said. "We can guess most of it. You married Virtue and let her keep house here so it would look respectable—throw off anybody who might be looking for you. The only thing I don't understand is how come you got this near and didn't go after the loot?"

"Damn heavy, that's why." He was still speaking with great difficulty, gasping painfully between words and phrases. "No way to sneak it out by wagon or pack train . . . somebody sure to notice. Had to wait. Till they built that railroad spur. Ship in small boxes . . . one at a time . . . right under all their noses. . . ."

"Well," said Doc gently, "you just got yourself rid of a heap of conscience, and I think you'll be glad you did as time goes on. So tell us where the loot is, Flood, and we'll do our best for you. I doubt you'll face any more charges after it's returned. Besides, we're getting you a doctor, fast as we can."

Flood shook his head. "Too late for that."

"I'll admit that wound's festered up something fierce," said Doc. "But you've still got a chance. Just tell us where you hid all that gold."

Flood nodded. He was breathing shallowly now, with harsh, gurgling sounds. "Right smack in the middle . . . pry up the stone . . . then dig. . ."

"Dig where?"

His lips moved silently as he tried to speak again.

Raider came forward. "Come on, Flood—where?"

"Under . . . the owl hoot. . . ."

"How's that?" asked Raider.

Flood's eyes became wide. He tried to lift his head, but it fell back again. Then it dropped to one side, with his lower jaw slack and his eyes still open. Open, but suddenly as lifeless as glass marbles.

CHAPTER SEVENTEEN

As nearly everybody in Tamarack Springs was exclaiming, in one way or another, it was the best Statehood Celebration ever.

The area around the corrals and holding pens of the stockyard, just outside of town, had been made into fairgrounds, with tents, tarpaulin canopies, and temporary shacks erected for the occasion and covered with streamers and bunting. In one corral, hands from nearby ranches were riding sun-fishing broncs and roping running calves to the cheers of the crowd. At another location there was a platform where a banjo and fiddle band was playing as a caller chanted out the figures for a group of square dancers.

Booths lined the approach to the fairgrounds, containing exhibits that would vie for prizes, which were being offered for everything, from the fattest hog to the tastiest jar of pickles. Ma Ormsby was in the food tent, with a number of other housewives, worrying a little because the fat Frenchman, Armand Sirois, had been appointed to the panel of judges, and she wasn't so sure the beef stew she'd concocted from her secret recipe would suit his fancy tastes.

Heather Ormsby, dressed like a female for a change in red-white-and-blue bombazine, was at the kissing booth, selling kisses with several other girls for two bits apiece, proceeds to go to the building of a new church with a genuine bronze bell in its steeple.

Near the entrance to all these festivities, Ab Ormsby had his new fire engine and water wagon on display. He sat on the vehicle glumly, his gold-braided uniform freshly pressed and his white chin whiskers neatly trimmed. Although the engine, repaired with the impeller the jeweler, Sam Ruby, had made, was once again in working order, and would be demonstrated later, hardly anyone was coming to look at it. After its failure to put out the schoolhouse fire, folks seemed to have lost confidence in it, and there was talk now of dissolving the fire department and releasing Ormsby from his duties.

As Ormsby regarded the milling crowd, which kept its distance from him, two Mexicans shuffled toward him. There was nothing unusual about them; Tamarack Springs had its share of Mexican field workers and ranch hands up from the border or the neighboring territories of Arizona and New Mexico. One seemed a bit tall for a Mexican, maybe, but they could grow as tall as anybody else on occasion, Ab told himself.

Both men wore serapes over their shoulders and broad-brimmed Jalisco sombreros that shaded their faces. They drew abreast of the fire engine. The shorter one, without lifting his head, said, "*Qué paso, jefe?*"

Ab thought he detected something familiar in the voice. He looked more closely as the man slowly brought his head up. In the shade of the big sombrero was the grinning face of Doc Weatherbee, its complexion darkened by some kind of stain, and its upper lip covered with a huge mustache, made from a bearskin Virtue had uncovered, to complete the disguise.

Ormsby stared. "What in hell are *you* two doin' here?"

"Long story, Ab," said Doc. "Let's hope there'll be time to tell it afterward. Too many things to do right now."

"If I was you, I'd skedaddle right out of town again.

You can't hide under them hats forever. And you're wanted for murder. I know you were set up—Heather told me all about it—but that don't change it.''

"We got to take our chances, Ab," said Raider. "And you're right about these duds. We found 'em in the restaurant in Yancy. I keep tellin' Doc I'm damned if we look like Mexicans, but there just wasn't any other way we could sneak in.''

Doc nodded. "Which we had to do. Because there's a question we've got to get answered. We figured you'd know the answer as well as anybody.''

"A question? You ain't makin' sense. What might the question be?''

"Ab," said Doc, "we can't tell you everything yet, but it's time to let you know who we really are. We're Pinkerton men and we've been here on an investigation all this time. If we find what we're looking for, it means you'll be rid of Winfield Brent once and for all, along with his pack of outlaws. He just won't have his big reason for sticking around any longer.''

"Now you're makin' even less sense.''

"Just answer the question if you can," Doc continued. "What do the words 'owl hoot' mean to you?''

"Owl hoot? Why, anybody knows what that means. When somebody's runnin' from the law, he's on the owl hoot, 'cause he moves at night, I reckon. The owl hoot trail. Just like you two are on right now.''

"What would it mean here in Tamarack Springs? Some kind of crick, or hill, or any other part of the landscape? There must be something around here known as the 'owl hoot.' ''

Ormsby shook his head. "Beats me. Maybe you should ask somebody who's been here longer. Rina Larkin might know.'' He waved in the general direction of the fairgrounds. "She's here somewhere. Hell, everybody is.''

"All right," said Doc. "We'll see if we can find her. Remember, not a word about seeing us here.''

Ormsby nodded, his face still wide open with bewilderment. Doc and Raider moved off, lowering the big hats over their faces again and keeping themselves beyond the edge of the crowd. Doc, who was something of an actor, had changed his gait into a leisurely shuffle, but Raider, somehow unable to get into the spirit of the thing, was taking his usual long, loping strides, scowling in the shade of the sombrero at the necessity of all this damn-fool masquerading.

"Why in hell don't we wait till dark?" asked Raider. "We can ride out to Rina Larkin's spread."

"The longer we wait, the more chance there is Brent'll locate that buried loot. He may know by now that Flood died in Yancy. Virtue was getting the hell out of there, pronto, after they buried her husband, but one of Brent's men could have tracked her down and made her talk. We don't know for sure, but we can't afford to ignore the possibility. If she mentioned that owl-hoot business, it might mean something to Brent. So we better find Rina right now if we can. Besides, Rina's got all those servants and ranch hands. They'd most likely spot us, and that way Brent or the marshal could find out we came back."

"Doc," said Raider, "you think so damn much you get yourself all tied up in knots."

Doc didn't bother to answer. They continued to amble along, never getting too close to the crowd, but peering at it closely from under their tilted hats. They passed the booth where Heather was dispensing kisses, but there were too many people around it for them to risk a nearer approach, and they kept walking.

At first they had no idea what was causing the sudden commotion that arose somewhere behind them. Hearing shouts, and sensing a stirring of the crowd, they turned to look back toward the fire engine. People seemed to be converging upon it. As far as they could make out, a rider had arrived and dismounted and was now in excited, earnest conversation with Ab Ormsby. In the next moment some of the shouts they were hearing coalesced into words.

"Fire!" someone cried.

"Whole damn town's afire!" yelled someone else.

Doc and Raider swung their gazes toward the town, a little downslope and less than half a mile away. A huge cloud of thick dark smoke was curling into the air, rolling like cabbage leaves as it rose, then bending into streaks in the wind.

The news was a fire in itself as it spread, crackling, across the fairgrounds. It was probably minutes, but it seemed only seconds, before dozens of fairgoers were racing toward the town, some mounted, some afoot, and some in the buggies or buckboards that had brought them. Doc and Raider scrambled toward their own horses, which they had left tethered to a fence rail near the fire engine. They no longer bothered to camouflage themselves—every eye was on the town and not upon two stray *paisanos* who were racing with everybody else.

The volunteer firemen were bringing themselves pell-mell to the fire engine and the water wagon, which Ormsby, with the help of bystanders, was quickly hitching to the horses. Armand Sirois, in a fancy tailcoat, with the rosette and ribbon of an official judge on its lapel, had also bustled up to the site to lend his services. As always when there was a need for haste, the horses were suddenly reluctant to be hitched and were snorting and trying to sidestep away from the whiffletrees.

As Doc and Raider, riding hard, neared the town, the smoke came toward them in thin waves and bit at their nostrils. When they reached the main street, with a milling crowd of horses and men in front of them, they saw the heart of the fire and were able to measure its extent. Flames leapt upward from the wooden buildings west of the Grand Palace. Four or five seemed to be burning now, but the wind was already spreading the conflagration to the structures beyond them. The smoke along the street was thick and acrid, and the immense heat of the fire kept anyone from approaching it too closely.

Some men were already at the horse trough in front of the grain and feed store, using buckets fetched from the hardware store in futile efforts to splash water toward the edge of the fire. The flames licked and swirled in an angry dance and, carried by the wind, reached out like lashing red whips for the adjacent buildings.

The crowd began to back away from the spreading fire; Doc and Raider, angling their horses away, stayed some distance from the edge of it.

At last the fire engine, drawn by four galloping horses and with Ormsby on its high seat desperately working the reins, charged down the main street, scattering the crowd, and came to a halt before the now burning grain and feed store. Ormsby leapt down from the contraption as the water wagon pulled up behind it. Sirois, squatting by the boiler, had already furiously stoked its embers with wood and was manipulating valves to bring up the pressure on the gauges. Volunteer firemen ran the suction hose to the water wagon as Ormsby and another assistant rolled the discharge hose from its big spool and pointed the long brass nozzle toward the fire.

"Let 'er rip!" yelled Ormsby.

Sirois turned a valve handle and a thick stream of water spurted out toward the fire. It curved through the air in a shallow arc that reached a good fifty feet or more, and when it struck the flames, steam arose with hissing and choking sounds that blended in with the crackling roar of the fire.

Neither Doc nor Raider knew much about the right and wrong ways to put out a fire, but they sensed—as did everyone in the crowd—that Ab Ormsby was doing it with great skill, and knew his business thoroughly. They dismounted and stepped a little nearer to the crowd, peering intently, fascinated by the way the flames were diminishing under the probing stream Ormsby laid upon them. The time passed swiftly, and when only an hour or a little more had gone by, there were suddenly no more flames; instead, charred walls and caved-in roofs from which smoke and steam were still rising. A bucket brigade, now able to work nearer to the cooling fire, moved in to supplement the hose and throw water on the last of the embers.

Doc and Raider had also come closer to the fire. They were not yet in the crowd of men who had been fighting it, but they were now only a few steps beyond it, their attention caught and held fast by the proceedings. It was Raider who suddenly sensed that something was wrong. He noticed some of the volunteer firemen glancing briefly at something behind Doc and Raider—glancing as though wondering about it mildly and in passing—and while this was a small sign, which might well have been missed, Raider was used to spotting small signs on the trail: Brush bent the wrong way, a bird in sudden flight when all else was still, or leaves stirring in a breeze when there was no breeze.

With this thought—or maybe an instant before it became a thought—Raider turned casually and looked at what should have been the empty street in back of Doc and himself.

"Doc!" he said quietly.

Doc also turned.

The riders were abreast, spread across the street, blocking it. They were perhaps twenty yards distant, pulled to a halt in a shallow crescent—a line that could be drawn in, like a net, upon Doc and Raider, where they stood. With no time for an exact count, Doc and Raider estimated that they numbered more than twenty men. They recognized many of them. The chinless Gouch was among them, along with his cohorts who had attempted to dry-gulch Doc and Raider; among the others were several habitués of the Grand Palace saloon they knew to be fugitives from the law.

Dan Carver, his wolfish eyes hard on Raider and Doc,

was in the center of the line. Beside him on a large white stallion sat Winfield Brent, posing in the saddle as though he were on parade, striking a handsome figure and evidently well aware of it.

Guns were pointed at Raider and Doc. Only one of the men in line was weaponless, and this was the man Raider had winged in the cottonwood grove. His injured arm was in a sling, and with his free hand he carried a coiled manila rope, thicker than a three-eighths lariat line. Its dangling end had been fashioned into a hangman's knot.

All of this registered instantly with Doc and Raider as they turned to look. Raider's immediate reaction was to reach for his side.

"Easy, Rade!" muttered Doc. "All these folks . . ."

Raider understood. The spectators were bunched behind them, and a sudden volley from Brent's line of outlaws might send bullets into their midst.

"Besides," added Doc, "our guns are in the saddlebags."

Raider remembered. Doc had reminded him that *paisanos* didn't ordinarily carry belts and holsters of hand-tooled leather containing expensive hand irons, pointing out that this would detract from their disguises.

Brent, who had been holding his thin smile upon them, now spoke, raising his voice for everyone in the crowd to hear. "There they are, folks! The two who shot down poor Dillard in cold blood! Thought they'd pass as Mexicans, but one of my men spotted 'em right away, while they were busy watchin' the fire. Wouldn't be surprised if they were the ones who started it!"

"Now, hold on," said Doc. "A trumped-up murder charge is bad enough, but lynching's going a little too far. It's time we cleared the air—right in front of everybody here!"

"I know you're fond of talkin', Doc," said Brent, "but it won't do you any good this time. You two are goin' to hang for what you did, and we don't need a trial you could wiggle out of. I've kept this town peaceable for a long time, and it's goin' to stay that way.''

Doc took a quick look at the townsmen behind himself and Raider. They had all dropped whatever they were doing and were listening intently, most of their eyes uneasy as they realized that at any moment bullets might be flying. Some were armed—a sixgun was part of dressing up for the celebration, after all—but none, as Rina Larkin had once pointed out, were gunmen in the professional sense. Most, over the years, had accepted Brent's way of keeping the town quiet, not liking the outlaw population in their midst, but still not quite ready to change what had always been, and what seemed to work well enough.

Doc faced Brent again. "We've got a jury right here," he said, "and it's time they heard a few facts."

"The facts are plain enough," said Brent. "Move real slow, you two. I want to see any weapons you've got under those colorful blankets of yours on the ground. Drop 'em real carefully, gentlemen.''

"Not before we present our case," Doc answered blandly. Raider glanced at him. He knew Doc had a way of throwing up talk as a smokescreen, which, in moments of danger, often gave them time to find a way out, but it still irritated him. "Raider beat Dillard to the draw, all right, but he shot for his leg. One of your men got him with a rifle—the way you planned it. His shot sounded like an echo, I expect. Then you hauled Raider into that cellar and had Turk work on him. Nobody seems to be wondering why. Well, it's showdown time, Brent—and now they're going to learn why.''

"I'm not goin' to debate with you, Weatherbee," said Brent, "so don't make up any wild stories. A man'll say anything to save his neck, and everybody here knows it.''

"We'll let them decide on who's bending the truth," said Doc. "That's what a jury's for.'' He turned and swung his eyes over the crowd again. "You've all heard, I expect, how a man named William Flood took a million dollars in gold from the Denver mint some years ago. What you don't know is that he buried it here somewhere—right in Tamarack Springs. Brent's been waiting all these years for Flood to come back and lead him to it. He thought maybe Flood had sent us after it, and that's why he set us up.''

''The man's loco!'' Brent called to the crowd. ''Come on, clear out—so nobody gets hurt.''

Ab Ormsby, who had been standing near the fire engine with the long brass nozzle in his hand, suddenly spoke up. ''Loco, hell!'' he said in his bellowing voice. ''I think it's like Doc says it is, and I think if we take the trouble we can prove it! Listen, everybody! It's time we stood up to these polecats. They been runnin' things around here long enough.''

Brent fixed a cold eye on Ormsby. ''You want to make a war out of it, Ab? I wouldn't advise that. There's not a man here who can stand up to my friends and associates here. And I don't want to see a massacre any more than they do.''

There was a long moment of silence as townsmen and ranch hands in for the celebration glanced nervously at each other. There were expressions of doubt on many of their faces, but none seemed willing to move. Brent's line of horsemen—nearly all of them gunslingers—was just too formidable, even to those who were beginning to suspect that Doc might be telling the truth.

At a nod from Brent, Dan Carver, the chinless Gouch, and two other men dismounted and came forward. Doc and Raider exchanged glances. In their silent way each agreed to what they were both thinking now. There was no more hope. There was nothing—absolutely nothing—they could do to resist. Not at the moment. And maybe not in any of the moments to come. Unless there was a miracle. Unless, for example, a bolt of lightning should come out of the clear blue sky and seek out only the men who now meant to hang them. Doc and Raider had their superstitions, but belief in avenging bolts of lightning wasn't one of them.

Within seconds they had been searched and their arms were bound to their sides. Carver reached forward and ripped away Doc's false mustache. Their own horses were brought forward, and Doc and Raider were lifted upon them. While this was being done, and while the remaining outlaws kept their guns pointed and a wary eye on the crowd, two other men looped the hanging rope over a *viga*, or polelike beam, that extended from the roof of the adobe-style bank building across the street.

"You first, Weatherbee," Brent called to Doc. "Then we won't have to put up with that blabbermouth of yours while we're takin' care of your partner."

Doc's horse was led under the beam. They dropped the noose on his neck, and Carver tightened it. The crowd watched, wide-eyed, horrified, but, in some perverse way, fascinated. One slap on the horse's rump and Doc would be dangling, his neck broken, his legs twitching while he died.

Doc looked at Raider, and, for the first time since Raider had known him, some of the fear he felt was in his eyes. "Oh, shit," said Doc.

Raider nodded. That seemed to him as good a pair of last words as any.

Carver raised his hand to slap the horse and send it forward.

CHAPTER EIGHTEEN

Ab Ormsby was staring helplessly at the proceedings along with everybody else. He hadn't moved since he had spoken, though his chin whiskers were working back and forth with a cud-chewing motion—a sign that Ab was thinking and thinking hard. As the noose was being slipped on Doc's neck, he turned and looked at Armand Sirois, whose blubbery form was still crouched at the boiler of the fire engine, and who had been gaping at everything in bewilderment, his little rosebud lips trembling like those of an infant who had just been surprised with a slap on the bottom.

He caught the Frenchman's eye. With his own lips he formed the words, "Get ready!" Sirois nodded, and Ormsby hoped to hell he'd really understood.

He turned away from the Frenchman now and pointed the long nozzle of the fire hose at the line of riders with their drawn weapons.

"Let 'er rip!" roared Ab.

Sirois yanked at the valve handle, swinging it all the way. Water spurted from the hose with the force of a cannon shot, all but knocking Ormsby flat as he struggled to hold the whiplashing nozzle.

The stream of water struck the line of mounted men, dropping three of them from their horses immediatley and sending even the horses staggering back. Seeing the nozzle bucking in Ormsby's hands, the volunteer who had been assisting him when the fire was burning rushed to his side to help him steady it. Ormsby swung the gushing stream, playing it over the other riders, unhorsing several more and scattering the rest. The surprise was complete; the riders, wet and sputtering, were in a state of absolute confusion. Some who hadn't dropped their guns tried a few wild shots, none of which found a target.

And something happened to the bystanders. It was like the single impulse that passes through a flock of birds, making them all change direction at the same time. Seeing the outlaws suddenly this vulnerable, with their guns no longer pointed at the crowd, the townsmen and ranch hands rushed forward and sprang upon them. Pent-up fury was emerging; it was something everybody had been secretly wanting to do for a long time.

The melee that now followed would long be remembered in the town of Tamarack Springs as the best part of that year's Statehood Celebration. The ranch hands who had come to town had expected a few friendly fights, but this was more and better excitement than any had dreamed of. Within moments a number of them were slugging it out with the disarmed outlaws—and, on the whole, getting the better of them. An occasional shot sounded, fired by those outlaws who hadn't dropped their guns, and by ranch hands who had found the courage to draw, but the fracas was primarily a slugfest, with outlaws either borne to the ground by groups of men who overwhelmed them or bowled over with swinging punches or knees to the groin. The ranch hands, like ranch hands anywhere, were not experienced gunmen, but when it came to this kind of brawling they were in their element. Fists flew, heads butted chins, and some outlaws were picked up bodily, then slammed upon the ground.

It took a moment for Doc and Raider, in their saddles, to realize what was happening. In that same moment,

Carver and his men whirled their heads to see what was going on. They had been busy readying Doc for his hanging, and had holstered their guns. Men rushed toward them and crashed into them before they could draw. One man scurried to Doc's side and hacked at his bonds with a knife; the moment Doc's hands were free, he reached up and removed the noose from his neck, desperately hoping the cayuse under him wouldn't shy or leap forward before it was done. Luck was with him—about time for a touch of luck, Doc figured—and the horse, though sidestepping a bit, refrained from taking off and leaving him dangling. Immediately, Doc edged the animal toward Raider's horse, and began fumbling at the ropes that held his partner.

Winfield Brent was a little like Raider in one respect. He could size up a situation, without too much conscious thinking, in the time it took a rattlesnake's tongue to flicker, and that was what he did now. As his riders were being unhorsed by the powerful stream of water, and as the townsmen were rushing toward them, he knew immediately that Ab Ormsby had indeed turned this confrontation into a battle, and that the battle was already lost. He whirled his white stallion, turned it away from the melee, and rode hell-bent toward the edge of town.

Raider, his bonds removed, was swinging his arms to restore the circulation when he saw the big white horse, now at least a hundred yards off, about to disappear in the rolling hills to the south, where the trail to Yancy lay. He heeled the flanks of the somewhat scrubby roan under him and loose-reined its head, putting it into the gallop it had probably wanted to take all along to get away from the milling confusion in the main street. It surged forward, with Raider lightly balanced in the stirrups and his eyes straight ahead, hard upon Brent and his stallion.

By the time Raider reached the first low rise Brent was no longer in sight, though there was a stirring of dust in the trail where he had just been. Raider said, ''Whoa, horse,'' and pulled up short. He patted the animal's neck. ''You ain't gonna catch a stallion like that,'' he said to it, ''so there's no use makin' you try.''

He turned the roan, whose flanks were now sweat-covered, and headed it back toward the town. The road here passed through a shallow draw, the ridge on one side formed by an outcropping of rock along which grew a line of stunted, twisted junipers.

A shot sounded.

The horse whinnied, lurched to one side, and then fell, with Raider leaping from it to keep from being crushed under its weight. He saw the bullet hole and the spreading blood where a slug had struck it in the neck. On his hands and knees in the dust, Raider almost started to reach for his side, then instantly realized that his gun was in the saddlebag under the horse. At the same time he was peering at the junipers, trying to pick out the exact spot the shot had come from.

The white horse he had been pursuing rose from behind the line of rocks. Winfield Brent was still on it, sitting tall and easy, a Colt .45 raised and ready in his hand.

Brent came down the slope of the draw. He pointed the gun at Raider, who was now rising to his feet. Oddly, he seemed unwrinkled and without sweat after his hard ride as he sat there, striking what under other circumstances would have been a handsome equestrian pose.

''All I had to do was circle back, Raider,'' he said, almost pleasantly. ''You never figured I would, did you?''

Raider stared back at him evenly. ''Looks like you admire the sound of your own voice as much as Doc, Brent. Smartest thing you can do right now is put down that hogleg and figure on ridin' back. Take your medicine. Better than tryin' to run off and gettin' hunted down.''

''Raider,'' said Brent, ''I can kill you right now. With all the trouble you gave me, I really should. And I might, at that, unless you use your head for a change. Let's take a minute to talk, Raider. Cards on the table, for a change.

The first chance you've got to live a little longer is to tell me who you really are. You're a lawman from somewhere, aren't you?''

"Sort of," Raider said. "Pinkerton Agency. That explain things for you?''

"It does, indeed. But I believe you've a little more to tell. You must have more than a passin' idea where Flood buried all that gold—or you wouldn't have risked comin' back. Am I right?''

Raider tried to keep his face as bland as Doc could make his when he was talking to keep from getting shot. He already suspected what was on Brent's mind—and if it was what he thought, there just might be a later chance to catch Brent off guard. "Maybe I do know somethin' more you'd like to hear. Maybe you figure the two of us could join up and split the loot two ways, is that it?''

"That's exactly it," said Brent. "We shouldn't be lockin' horns, Raider; we're both a cut above the rest. I'm a man who never lets anything stand in my way, and I believe you are, too. Let me tell you a few things *you* might not know about, just so we know where we stand. I got word that Flood showed up in Yancy and died there from a slug in his side. It's my guess you saw him before he died. And, since you *did* return to the Springs, he must have told you something. I have to admit I didn't see this right away, or I wouldn't have put together a lynchin' party. But it came to me just now, while I was ridin' off, and that's why I circled back.''

As Brent talked, Raider casually edged a little closer to him. Brent, busy talking, didn't seem to be spooked by it. "All right, Brent," he said. "Maybe you're makin' sense, after all. Flood did say somethin'. Which I can't figure out—but maybe you can. There's just one thing that bothers me a little here. If I tell you what it was, what's to keep you from shootin' off that gun and leavin' me here in the dust?''

"You have a point," said Brent. He holstered his gun.

"That ain't good enough," said Raider. "Take the belt off and hang it behind the saddle, where you can't get to it fast."

"Very well," said Brent, complying. "Now, what did Flood say?"

"Somethin' about pryin' up the rocks. Under the owl hoot, he said."

Brent's finely cut eyebrows rose immediately. "Of course!" he said. "That's where it was all the time!"

"What's it mean, Brent? What in hell's the 'owl hoot'?"

"Gunslingers are somethin' like cowhands. When they get together and relax they give their own names to things. Like thieves havin' their own language, so outsiders won't tumble to what they're sayin'. Sometimes these names last and sometimes they don't. Hardly anybody remembers now what 'owl hoot' meant when Flood first came to the Springs."

Brent's hand was sliding back toward the gunbelt now, and Raider, expecting this, didn't miss it. He moved himself forward another foot or two. "Never mind the history lesson," he said. "What's it mean?"

"It was their name for the whorehouse, Raider. 'Under the owl hoot.' In the cellar, under those flagstones. Flood was always hangin' around the whorehouse, and he must've had plenty of time to put it there."

Brent's talk, as Raider knew very well, was now meant as camouflage. His hand was still easing toward the gunbelt. This was the one moment in which Raider could make his play with a chance that it might succeed. He sprang forward. Brent's hand closed on the gunbelt and he whipped it around in front of him, digging for the holstered weapon.

If Raider had reached Brent a split second later, the gun, going off, would have caught him full in the face. But he got his hand under it as he crashed into the side of the white stallion and deflected its barrel upward. The stallion shied at the sound of the shot. In the same instant, Raider grabbed Brent, who was off balance, and pulled him down from the saddle.

The two men rocked back and forth, struggling, Raider's hand now closed on Brent's wrist, twisting it to keep the gun pointed off to one side. Suddenly Raider brought his knee up hard into Brent's groin. Brent gasped with pain and staggered back, dropping the gun. Raider shoved him all the way back, dove for the gun, and was on his feet again before Brent could get back to him. Brent saw the gun leveled at his gut and wisely came to a halt.

There was a stretch of silence as both men faced each other, Brent bent over a little with his hand on his aching groin, Raider upright, his chest heaving slightly as he caught his breath again.

"We're walkin' back to town, Brent," Raider finally said. "Never liked walkin' much, but this time I reckon I can stand it."

CHAPTER NINETEEN

"I'm glad to see you, Raider," said Rina Larkin. "I've been waiting for you to get here."

She turned and led the way into the living room.

Outside the ranch house the night had drawn a studded blanket of stars over the sky. In a nearby creek somewhere frogs were whistling a mating song.

Rina had come to the door in her transparent silky peignoir with the ostrich feathers curling up from its collar. Under it the full curves of her figure were clearly visible, and the heavy perfume she wore gave off a musky scent that tugged at Raider's nostrils.

Raider wore a clean white placket shirt with billowing sleeves, and he was freshly bathed and shaven, with even his broad mustache neatly trimmed. He stood there quietly in the dimly lit room as Rina turned gracefully and faced him.

Her smile floated across her broad red lips. She touched the neck of her robe, pulling it apart a little, to show more of her billowing, creamy breasts, leaving the nipples still partly concealed by the diaphanous material.

"We're alone tonight, Raider," she said. "Finally. I've sent everyone into town. For a while, I wondered if you'd be able to get away. There's been so much going on since they dug up all that gold."

Raider nodded. He and Doc had been busy as weasels in a henhouse, that was for sure. With Winfield Brent and Dan Carver and more than twenty wanted fugitives in custody, they'd had to help the town officials figure out who should get extradited, and who should go to trial— and for what—and get out reports for the Pinkerton home office that were enough to give a man cramps in his shooting hand. To say nothing of organizing a twenty-four-hour guard on the gold coins in their ammunition boxes until the government men arrived. The last Raider had heard, a whole troop of cavalry was being sent.

Rina now pirouetted toward the sideboy to pour Raider some Tennessee whiskey. She made a dance figure out of it, putting all of her solid, fleshy curves into sinuous motion, in effect showing Raider what he could look forward to in just a moment. "You're going to stay on as marshal, aren't you? Everybody wants you to."

" 'Fraid not." Raider shook his head. "Doc and I'll be driftin' back soon as everything gets squared away."

She came back with his tumbler of whiskey, leaning toward him as she handed it to him, letting him breathe in her womanly aura, watching him closely to see the first flames of his excitement as she kindled it. "Stay, Raider," she said. "I've told you what you and I can do together. We'll own the town—we'll own everything. And you know what else I can do for you—or have you forgotten already?"

Raider frowned and sipped his whiskey. "You set them fires, didn't you, Rina?" he said quietly.

"What?" Her eyebrows formed little arches of surprise.

"It took some doin' to find out by telegraph, but once we did it all fell into place. Doc understands it better'n I do, but what it boils down to is those insurance policies. First, the regular delay while the insurance company looks for reasons not to pay off. Then, since they get paid by the town itself, once the town collects, another long delay you could control by bein' on the town council and havin' a big say in everything. Could be as long as a year before anybody collected. Most couldn't hold out that long and went outa business, or had to sell their property. Real cheap. To you, Rina, and every little parcel you picked up brought you that much nearer to ownin' the whole damn town. A good investment, like you say. Big as Denver or Chicago one o' these days.''

"Raider! What's come over you? What are you talking about?"

"A lotta things," said Raider. "The way you covered your tracks. You burned a few public buildings like the town hall and the schoolhouse along with the private property you were after, just to throw anybody off who might start guessin' things. Or maybe some o' them just caught fire 'cause they were nearby. Anyway, you're the firebug, Rina; I'd of figured it out long ago if there hadn't been so damn much else on my mind.''

"If I wanted everything to burn down why did I help bring that fire engine here?"

"To put on a show, I reckon. Make 'em all believe you were the ramrod when it came to buildin' up the town. And Brent went along with you without knowin' it when he tried to keep that fire engine from ever gettin' here. It was Brent, as a matter of fact, who started Doc and me thinkin' about all this. When he made a full confession to everything he did. Not for the sake of his conscience—he ain't got one. He's figurin' on some kind of a deal so he doesn't get put away the rest of his unnatural life, and comin' clean makes him look better—or so he figures, I reckon. Point is, while he was confessin' to everything else in the book, he insisted, real firm, that he never set those fires. Seemed to Doc and me he might just be tellin' the truth for a change.''

"You'd take the word of a man like Brent, and turn around and accuse *me*? You're stark, raving mad, Raider.''

"Like hell I am. Let me finish. Just one more little thing—what finally told me it had to be you. Somethin' you said to me once, and I didn't pay much attention to it at the time, but there it was, in my craw, itchin' all along like a burr under the saddle. When Doc and I started tryin' to untangle the whole mess, I suddenly remembered it.''

"Really?" she said coldly. "And what was that?"

"The night you were givin' me all those—uh—good reasons to throw in with you and stick around. Tellin' me how you'd noticed I could take care o' myself. How Doc and I stood up to the gunslingers, and then how we kept ourselves from gettin' ambushed the night we were pokin' around in the ruins of the town hall. That was real sweet talk, Rina, and I got to admit I enjoy bein' admired by a whole bundle of woman as well as the next man. But you slipped up, Rina—made a mistake. You see, Doc and I never told another soul about that ambush. The only other person who could know was the one who shot at us. And whoever did figured we might come up with evidence of arson, so he—or she, as it turns out now—had to be the one who set the fires.''

Rina stared at him expressionlessly for a drawn-out moment. "You're going to have a hard time proving any of this, Raider."

"Reckon so." He shrugged. "Maybe it never will get proved—not for a court of law, anyway. That's up to the lawyers and such who'll be comin' to town. Doc and I, we did our part of the job and we'll be long gone by then."

"Raider—"

"Yeah?"

Her eyes were switching like cat's tails. "I don't think you'll stir up this hornet's nest. I don't think you'll make all this trouble for me. Not when you remember what I'm going to give you right now."

She drew apart the folds of her shimmering robe slowly. The globes of her immense breasts were revealed, their hardened nipples firm and upright in the nests of pink flesh that surrounded them. The robe slipped over her broad shoulders and dropped away, so that she stood before him naked, her hips curving out in ample, sweeping lines from her tiny waist, her full-fleshed thighs seeming to quiver as they drew themselves down from the luxurious, cushioned patch of dark hair on the resilient mound that contained her quim. She came forward, slid her arms around Raider's neck, and pressed herself into him. She reached down and curled her fingers around the lump in Raider's trousers. The lump grew.

Raider tried to keep his voice steady. "That ain't gonna do you no good, Rina."

"Going to turn it down, Raider? It's better than you'll get anywhere else. You know that."

"I never turn anything like this down," Raider said. "But after it's over I'm still turnin' you in for settin' those fires."

"Really?" Rina moved backward, pulling Raider toward the divan. "Let me set *you* on fire, Raider; I think you'll change your mind."

"Go ahead. Just don't expect anything."

"I'll take my chances, Raider," she said. "At the very least, I'll have something I can remember for a while."

"Me, too, I reckon," Raider said, reaching into her parted negligee to cup his hand around one burgeoning, creamy breast, its great nipple now hardening to the bursting point.

J.D. HARDIN

"THE MOST EXCITING WESTERN WRITER SINCE LOUIS L'AMOUR"
—JAKE LOGAN

_____ 0-867-16840	BLOOD, SWEAT AND GOLD	$1.95
_____ 0-867-16842	BLOODY SANDS	$1.95
_____ 0-867-16882	BULLETS, BUZZARDS, BOXES OF PINE	$1.95
_____ 0-867-16877	COLDHEARTED LADY	$1.95
_____ 0-867-21101	DEATH FLOTILLA	$1.95
_____ 0-867-16911	DEATH LODE	$1.95
_____ 0-867-16843	FACE DOWN IN A COFFIN	$1.95
_____ 0-867-16844	THE GOOD, THE BAD, AND THE DEADLY	$1.95
_____ 0-867-21002	GUNFIRE AT SPANISH ROCK	$1.95
_____ 0-867-16799	HARD CHAINS. SOFT WOMEN	$1.95
_____ 0-867-16881	THE MAN WHO BIT SNAKES	$1.95
_____ 0-867-16861	RAIDER'S GOLD	$1.95
_____ 0-867-16883	RAIDER'S HELL	$1.95
_____ 0-867-16767	RAIDER'S REVENGE	$1.95
_____ 0-867-16839	SILVER TOMBSTONES	$1.95
_____ 0-867-21133	SNAKE RIVER RESCUE	$1.95
_____ 0-867-21039	SONS AND SINNERS	$1.95
_____ 0-867-16869	THE SPIRIT AND THE FLESH	$1.95
_____ 0-425-06001-2	BIBLES, BULLETS AND BRIDES	$2.25